The rough baritone stroked her quivering nerves even as her eyes went wide when she saw him without an apron for the first time. The ink-blue cotton sleeveless t-shirt he wore fitted across his wide and muscular chest as if he had been poured into it, his stomach as flat as a washboard. She clenched her left fist, her hold on the coffee mug tightening as she curbed the sudden urge to caress his well-honed biceps. Her mouth dried up, parching her throat as well before she took a quick gulp of the scalding coffee, her eyes continuing to travel over the cream cotton pants which stretched over the length of his muscular legs. His feet were encased in black sneakers with a neon yellow trim. She didn't miss the bare ankles on show between the hem of the pants and the shoes as it was obvious he wore no socks. All this she noticed in the span of a few seconds, feeling a desperate urge to fan herself as her blood sizzled, making her sweat despite the cool weather.

ABOUT THE AUTHOR

Sundari Venkatraman is an Indie Author who has 69 books to her credit. These books have consistently featured in the Top 100 Bestseller Lists on Amazon Kindle, in both romance as well as Asian Drama categories. Her latest hot romances have all been on #1 Bestseller slot in Amazon India for over a month.

TAURUS TEMPTATION is a hot romance novel and the third book in the Written in the Stars series. It can also be read as a standalone novel. This kindle book remained in the #1 Bestseller position on Amazon India for three months after its release.

Even as a child, Sundari absolutely loved the 'lived happily ever after' syndrome and she grew up on a steady diet of fairy tales, Phantom comics, and Mandrake comics. It was always about good triumphing over evil and a happy ending after the protagonists surmounted all unexpected obstacles.

Once she entered her teens, Sundari switched her loyalties from fairy tales to Mills & Boon. While she loved reading both, she kept visualising what would have happened if there were similar situations happening in India; to local heroes and heroines. And of course, the joy of vanquishing the ubiquitous evil villains! Her imagination soared and she happily ensconced herself in a rosy romantic cocoon for many years.

Then came the writing—a true bolt from the blue! And Sundari Venkatraman has never looked back.

Books by Sundari Venkatraman

Standalone novels
The Malhotra Bride
Meghna
The Madras Affair
An Autograph for Anjali
Twin Torment
Finding Anya
Mr. Perfect
Man Friday
Her Prince Charming
Love in Agartha
Arjun's Penance
The Floundering Author
Ryan Finds a Bride
Tinder Loving Care
Shaan Gets Hitched
For Better or For Worse
Love… No Conditions Asked
Is This Love?
Press Restart

Collection of shorts
Matches Made in Heaven
Tales of Sunshine

Marriages Made in India Series
#1 The Runaway Bridegroom
#2 Her Smitten Husband
#3 His Drunken Wife
#4 Her Secret Husband
#5 The Casanova's Wife
#6 Her Bohemian Husband

The Bansal Legacy Trilogy
#1 Simha International
#2 Rose Garden International
#3 Maharaja International

The Thakore Royals Trilogy
#1 The Marriage Predicament
#2 Tied in Knots
#3 The Wooing of the Shrew

The Groom Series Trilogy
#1 Groomnapped
#2 Gobsmacked
#3 Grounded

Written in the Stars Series
#1 Scorpio Superstar
#2 Leo's Desire
#3 Taurus Temptation
#4 Virgo's Krush
#5 Libra's Flame
#6 Aquarius Rebel

Arora Iyers Trilogy
#1 Once Bitten Twice Lucky
#2 Heartthrob
#3 Call of the Heart

Dashavatar (Indian Mythology)
MATSYA: The First Avatar
KURMA: The Second Avatar
VARAHA: The Third Avatar
NARASIMHA: The Fourth Avatar
VAMANA: The Fifth Avatar
PARASHURAMA: The Sixth Avatar

**The Princess Series
(Historical Romance)**
#1 The Passionate Princess
#2 The Rebel Princess

**The Prince Series
(Historical Romance)**
#1 The Banished Prince

The Writer's Toolkit (Non-fiction)
Publishing Your Book on Amazon KDP

Bollywood Bros Trilogy
#1 Sing For Me
#2 Dance With Me
#3 Lights, Camera, Action!

Romantic Shorts
#1 *Chahti Hoon Tumhe*
#2 Beauty is but Skin Deep
#3 Madeinheaven.com
#4 An Arranged Match
#5 The Reluctant Bride
#6 *Shweta ka Swayamvar*
#7 Papa's Girl
#8 Red Rose Dating Agency
#9 Rahat Mili
#10 Reema's Matchmakers
#11 The Matchmaker's Dream

TAURUS TEMPTATION

WRITTEN IN THE STARS
BOOK 3

A romance novel by
SUNDARI VENKATRAMAN

FLAMING SUN

Notion Press Media Pvt Ltd
No. 50, Chettiyar Agaram Main Road,
Vanagaram, Chennai, Tamil Nadu – 600 095

First Published by Flaming Sun 2020
Printed & Distributed by Notion Press
Copyright © Sundari Venkatraman 2020 & 2024
All Rights Reserved.

ISBN 979-8-89498-021-8

Edited by: The Book Club Editorial Panel
Beta read by: Rubina Ramesh
Cover Illustration: Unaiza Merchant

On the Taurus-Cancer match…

Imagine you are a huge rock, sitting high on top of a mountain. Nothing frightens you, or moves you. You're so tough, the storms of thousands of years haven't even scratched your surface, though they've worn away lesser rocks into helpless pebbles. Then one chilly day, an apparently harmless drop of water brightly splashes on you, and trickles its way into a deep crack in your centre, which has been there since you were born, but has been overlooked by the rains and winds until now.

What will you do?

You will do nothing. You, who have stood up against centuries of floods and tornados, have nothing to fear from one tiny drop of water. The next day, the thermometer drops to zero, and the drop of water freezes in your centre. The freezing causes it to expand, and the expansion hurts you. Since nothing has ever before been able to weaken your strength, how do you feel about a drop of water which is expanding inside you, and threatening to crack you in two?

A quiet little meditation like that will throw a great illumination on what it's like to be an earthy, invulnerable Taurus man in love with a watery, gentle and sometimes Looney Moon Cancer Maiden. It can shake him to his foundations. But it's too late. She's already penetrated the secret place no one else has ever quite reached—his heart. Since a Bull's heart is as strong as both his will and his back, he probably won't break in half. But he'll never again be the same, once this girl has enticed him to run along the beach under a midnight sky, in the zigzag directions of the Crab, crying and laughing—and feeling. Taurus knows all about touching, but feeling is a slightly different word. She'll teach him all its meanings and synonyms.

– LINDA GOODMAN

idyut Kamath stared at the engagement ring in the palm of his left hand, the diamonds sparkling in the light coming from the windows of the coffee shop he owned; glad that there was no one else on the first floor as the labourers were at work in the lower level.

He shook his head, still unable to wrap his head around the conversation he had just had with his fiancée. No, ex-fiancée Janani.

Janani Rai wasn't interested in marrying him, not any more. They had been engaged for six months and had been planning to tie the knot in the January of the coming year, which was still more than five months away. Her reason: Vidyut's change of career.

Earlier in the morning, he had woken up to see a message from his fiancée; yes, she had still been betrothed to him at that time.

I hv to mt u. urgnt.

A scowl had gathered on Vidyut's face. There was only a week to go before the opening he was planning for his coffee shop and there were a number of things which needed to be taken care of before that. He really didn't have the time now. But not seeing a way out of giving her his time, he sent his reply on WhatsApp.

Cm ovr to Kmth Kffe by 9.

From an old-fashioned and traditional Kannada family, Janani had decided to become a primary school teacher, considering the job as a stop gap before getting married and settling down with a family of her own.

The first three months of their engagement, after the match being fixed by their respective parents, the two of them could rarely meet due to Vidyut's hectic office hours at the MNC he worked. It was during that time when Vidyut had seriously considered quitting his job and setting up his own business. After all, he would never be able to give time to his wife if he continued to work such crazy hours at the MNC. Fascinated with the idea of owning and running a restaurant, and having a craze for coffee, he had come up with the plan of Kamath's Koffee. Not one to let the grass grow under his feet, he had drawn out a plan at the same time when he put in his papers.

While he loved and respected his father, Arun Kamath, it was his mother Vandana whom the Taurus totally adored. The old man, retired from his cushy job, had been insistent that his US-educated son should get a position with a big company which gave him a regular and exorbitant salary. After all, who wanted to take on the headache of running a business which was risky?

All hell had broken loose when Vidyut had finally informed his parents that he had quit his lucrative job to make time for setting up and running a—of all things—coffee shop.

"Are you mad?" Arun roared at the son he had adored until that moment. Just now, he was too angry with his firstborn. He jumped up from the sofa to glare at Vidyut, standing toe to toe with him, not caring for the idea of having to look up as the younger man was four inches taller. "How could you quit your job? They were paying you so handsomely too."

"*Appa…*"

"Don't *Appa* me, Vidu. How could you take such a decision without consulting me?"

"I am thirty, *Appa*. And I have lived an independent life for four years in the US. Why shouldn't I make my own decisions?" Vidyut tried to pacify his parent with his logic.

Vandana turned from one man to the other, an unhappy expression on her face. Before she could really savour her son's return from the USA, her husband had fixed Vidyut's marriage. Even she had been surprised that her son had agreed to the arranged match without raising too many objections. There had been many heated arguments between father and son before the marriage could be arranged was something Vandana had decided to forget.

Vidyut had agreed to the engagement on one condition—that the wedding should take place one whole year later. That was the least time he needed to get to know his future wife, Janani.

It had been another shocker to Vandana, her husband agreeing to the long engagement. And now this! Why couldn't she have a life of calm and quiet?

"Don't be ridiculous, Vidu. I am not saying you shouldn't make your own decisions. But this is not only your career we are talking about here, but your whole life, your future. You can't fool around with something you have worked so hard for." It was Arun's turn to cool down his temper and speak to his son placatingly; the effort almost suffocating him.

"Well, *Appa*. I have only one life to lead and I want to live it in a way that makes me happy. I…"

"You are being damn selfish, son." Arun began to shout again. "Did you think of your old parents? The woman you are engaged to? Your unborn children? You…"

"*Appa!*" Vidyut threw an arm around his father's shoulders to hug him. "What has my decision to open a coffee shop do with all of you?"

"Don't be a fool, Vidu. You will not see much money in this venture of yours. Even if money does trickle in, it won't be a fixed income. It is a major risk you will be taking." Arun was seriously worried, a frown bringing his pepper and salt eyebrows together as he spoke to his son in a pleading voice.

"Of course it will be a risk, *Appa*. But then, what's life without risk? Even my marriage to Janani will be a risk, wouldn't it? After all, I will be marrying a stranger."

"Shut up, Vidu. Who are you blaming for that? You wanted a year to get to know her better. If you had followed up, she wouldn't be a stranger to you today, would she?" Arun pinned his son with his sharp gaze, challenging him to come up with a convincing answer to that.

Vidyut shrugged. "Which is one of the many problems I am facing working for my company. The job is draining me out, *Appa*; both my time and my energy.

I just don't have enough of either to give to Janani. I haven't been able to spend time with her at all since the engagement."

"This is all nonsense. You should have taken my advice and married her immediately. It's not that late even now. Get married and get to know your wife all you want. That's how your mother and I got to know one another." There was a triumphant expression on his father's face as Arun advised Vidyut.

Vidyut shook his head slowly. "As I mentioned, it's just one of the problems. Another is that I hate my desk job, sitting in front of the computer and sorting out issues which aren't my own." He worked as a trouble shooter for his company and while he was extremely good at his job and well appreciated for the same, the work had begun to pall after the first few months. "I want to do something creative, *Appa,* while also being my own boss."

Arun turned to appeal to his wife. "Vandana, see what your son wants to do. He wants to give up a high-class job and become a cook." He smote his forehead. "It's all my bad karma. What else to say?!" He went into his bedroom and banged the door shut, leaving the mother and son in the living room.

"Vidu, why don't you listen to your father? He only means well."

"*Amma,* I am aware *Appa* means well." Vidyut grinned at her before hugging his mother. "But that is nowhere near enough for how I should live my life. This is a longstanding dream, *Amma.* And I have been saving up for this only. I've even bought the space for it."

"What? Really?" Vandana gave her son an astounded look. "So, why didn't you tell your father that you purchased property? It would have made him happy."

"Would it? I suppose you are right. But then, he would insist that I give it away on rent."

"That's true. Why don't you? It will be one more side income, Vidu. It's actually a good…"

"*Amma!*" Vidyut moved away from his mother to glare down at her. "Are you trying to convince me to give up the idea of running my own coffee shop?"

She gave a nod before shaking her head. "I don't know, Vidu. All I want is for you to be happy. And I want your father to be happy too. I…" She worried her lower lip as she looked at him appealingly.

"Was *Appa* unhappy when he worked as finance director for his company? He had started in the position of team leader and worked his way up in the same company for forty-two years. Did it make him happy or no?" Vidyut looked at his mother, waiting for her answer.

"He was very happy, Vidu. What kind of a question is that?" Vandana was bewildered.

"There! You had your one wish come true; that your husband should be happy. Right?"

She gave him a dubious nod, unsure about where this conversation was going. "That's true."

"You also want your son to be happy, right?" Vidyut's voice trembled with laughter as he cornered his mother with the question.

"That's right."

"I can only be happy if I have my own coffee shop. I even have a name for it—Kamath's Koffee. What do you think?" he asked her, giving her a wide grin.

"Will you be sitting at the billing counter and counting cash the whole day?" Vandana was trying hard to understand if that was what would make her son happy. She couldn't see anything creative in such an exercise though.

Vidyut laughed out loud, shaking his head at her. "No, *Amma*. I plan to employ half a dozen college students to do that. I will be in charge of the kitchen."

"What?" Vandana's mouth opened wide as she gazed at him with a stunned expression on her face. "You are going to be a cook?" Her husband had been right and no wonder he was angry. Had they sent their son to America to do his MBA so that he could become a measly cook? Even Vandana, with only her high school education, could manage that with one hand tied behind her back. That they employed a cook at home was another matter altogether.

"I will be in charge of the various coffee blends and baking. As for the rest, I have organised for two more chefs."

"How big is your coffee shop?" asked his mother, quickly counting the number of people he planned to employ. "And how are you going to pay the wages of eight people?"

"You are smart, *Amma*." Vidyut patted her cheek. "Not eight people, but nine, including me. Don't I get a salary?" he teased.

"So! Tell me how you are planning to go about it."

"By selling coffee, cakes, and a number of other food items. How else?"

"But won't it be difficult?" she asked, a worried frown on her face.

"Hmm… it won't be easy, *Amma*. But then, nothing comes easy in life. Definitely not the job with the MNC that pays a big, fat salary." He shrugged. "I will at least be doing something I love."

Vandana placed her hands on his cheeks and held his face lovingly. "I understand that you want to do this, Vidu. But I hope you realise that it's going to be difficult to bring your father around."

"Well, I've crossed the first hurdle by announcing my decision. Let's see how it goes." He wasn't going to worry too much. There was only one way to show his father that his business would do well; by actually opening the coffee shop and running it.

That Janani's parents didn't approve his choice either was just another bone that Vidyut's father had to pick.

"You are behaving very irresponsibly, Vidyut." The angry Arun used his son's full name, making his disapproval clear.

Vidyut looked up from his laptop, where he had been designing invitation cards to be sent to people by email and WhatsApp. "Why?" he asked.

"Haresh Rai phoned me today. Your father-in-law is not at all happy with the change in your career." Arun sighed extra-loudly.

Vidyut shrugged. "That's sad, *Appa*."

"Don't you feel bad that you are the reason for so many people's unhappiness?" asked his father.

"What?" Vidyut placed his laptop on the table to give his father his complete attention. "What does that even mean? Don't I have a right to be happy? Do what I want?" he asked, his temper simmering to the fore.

"Look at it from their view point, son. They believed they were getting a rich son-in-law who works in a high position with a big company. But now…"

"They will get a son-in-law who's going to create a big brand; who is also rich and who will have more time for their daughter. Wouldn't you call it a win-win situation?" Vidyut got up from the sofa to walk up and down the living room. He never knew he would face so much opposition to his pet project. But that only made him all the more determined, being the bull-headed Taurus that he was.

Arun opened his mouth and then closed it, tilting his head to the side as he looked at his son, his lips drooping at the corners. As if he had completely given up on Vidyut while being confident that his son's life was going to the dogs!

And then Janani had arrived at the coffee shop that morning…

"Hey, Jan. How are you?" Vidyut gave her a sunny smile, taking her hand in his and drawing her into the middle of the coffee shop.

Pulling her hand out of his hold, she gave him a nod, but there was no smile on her face. "I'm fine." Refusing to meet his gaze, she turned around to look at the large and airy space, complete with glass and wooden counters and display shelves, impressed in spite of herself. "So, this is your coffee shop."

"Yeah, it will be, once it's ready. But I am glad you could come today. There is also seating on the first floor. Before we go up, would you like some coffee?" he asked.

She shook her head. "I don't have much time really. My mother is expecting me in half an hour."

Vidyut grimaced. They rarely got an opportunity to spend private time together. The few times they had, Janani always insisted that either her mother or her father expected her to return home soon. Were they worried that the engaged couple might step out of line?

"In that case, let me get a cup for myself." He quickly went behind the counter and fetched himself a steaming mug. "Let's go upstairs where there's less noise." The carpenters were not quite finished with the furniture on the ground floor.

Janani looked around the first-floor area which was bright with sunlight pouring in through the floor-length windows along the whole length of one wall which looked out on the street.

There were tables and chairs for twos, fours, and sixes with enough space to walk around. As she quickly counted the chairs, Vidyut interrupted to say, "One hundred people can sit here and the same number downstairs."

"How do you plan to get so many customers?" she asked, turning around to pin him with her dark gaze.

"Huh?" He was surprised at the vehemence in her voice. He had never heard her uttering anything beyond monosyllables. "By careful and well-planned marketing. How else?"

"Aren't you taking a major risk?" she asked.

"Of course, I am."

"Isn't that foolish?"

Vidyut placed his coffee mug on a table with extra care, taking deep breaths to calm down his rising temper. "Isn't what foolish?" he asked in an ominous voice.

"Taking such a risk."

"I don't think so." He bit out the words.

"My parents think so. My father says that you are being extremely foolish by starting this coffee shop out of the blue. They had only agreed to a marriage between the two of us because you have a steady job with a big salary. Weren't you getting a fifty-lakh package per year? Anyway, they are extremely upset that you have given up your job. Is there a way you can get it back?"

Vidyut gritted his teeth until his jaw ached. He didn't want to say something to upset his young fiancée. And she was young at just twenty-six; four years younger than he was. "What about you? Do you think I am being foolish? Do you think I shouldn't take risks?"

She shook her head slowly. "I don't know. I've always lived by my parents' standards and I don't want to displease them."

"Tell me something, Jan. If I don't take risks at thirty, don't you think I will end up being a dead bore in the next decade or so?" he asked, a small smile on his face as he tried to lighten the situation. He could see that Janani probably felt torn between what he was doing and her parents' disapproval.

She looked at him dispiritedly, her lips drooping at the corners. Janani had led a smooth and uneventful life and had never stepped out of line, ever. Unlike Haasini, her younger sibling by four years. Haasini was the brat in the family; with both parents disapproving her behaviour. Janani would have hated to live like Haasini and earn her parents' wrath. She shuddered just thinking about her sister before taking a deep breath to calm herself down. Her father had been clear in his instructions. She had to somehow convince her fiancé to give up this foolish idea for a coffee shop and get back to work at the MNC.

"Vidyut, listen. I don't know anything about taking risks. Why bother when life is already going so smoothly? I hope I have a say in your life as your fiancée." She paused, waiting for his response.

"Maybe." Vidyut was cautious with his answer, wondering what she was getting at.

"I want you to return to your old job and give up this idea of running a coffee shop." She spoke quickly, repeating her father's words verbatim.

So, that's how it was going to be! "And if I don't do either?" he asked, his hands on his hips, his legs apart, his head tilted to one side; his whole stance challenging.

"Then I will have to break off our engagement." Janani removed the diamond ring from her left hand and placed it on the table where it caught the sunlight and winked at them both.

"Is this your final decision?" asked Vidyut, the colour leaving his face.

"Yes." She did an about turn and walked quickly down the stairs and out of the coffee shop.

Picking up the ring she had left behind, Vidyut stared at it unseeingly as he looked within himself.

Do I feel hurt? Or maybe even betrayed?

The answer came swiftly. Absolutely nothing. He felt completely indifferent. If Janani couldn't understand his dream, then she was definitely not the right partner for him.

He sighed. Explaining that to his parents, especially to his father, wasn't going to be easy. Picking the empty mug in his hand, he went down the staircase, taking the steps two at a time, a spring in his step as he felt a strange lightness in his heart for the first time since he got engaged.

Haasini Rai just managed to jump into the AC chair car of the train from Mysuru to Bengaluru before it left the platform at Mysuru Junction. Dragging her trolley case even as she adjusted the straps of her backpack, she walked into the compartment, looking to the left and then to the right as she searched for her seat number. It was towards the middle of the compartment, on the left side. Pushing her case under the seat, Haasini placed her backpack on the small foldable table, glad she had got herself a window seat.

She had booked herself on the train instead of a bus so that she could work comfortably on her laptop. But somehow, once she boarded, she didn't have the heart to remove her laptop from her backpack.

Shutting her eyes, she leaned back in the seat, her mind running over the time she had spent in Mysuru.

Haasini felt old and wise at the tender age of twenty-two and three months. It was two years and a month till date from the time she had stolen out of her home in Bengaluru in the middle of the night to run away with Yeshwant Sharma on his motorbike, all the way to his flat in Mysuru. He had promised her the usual things—marriage and security.

But the Cancerian woman had been seeking neither marriage nor security. She was keen on adventure, having fun, anything out of the ordinary in her humdrum life. At twenty, Haasini had not considered the magnitude or the repercussions of her actions.

She had been attracted to the good-looking Yeshwant and it was so thrilling that an older man—he was twelve years her senior—was paying her attention. Yeshwant had been visiting his cousin sister and her family who were next door neighbours to the Rai family.

Haasini had met Yeshwant a few times and had decided he was the man for her when her blood sizzled with chemistry. It hadn't been difficult for him to persuade her to run away with him. Yeshwant had known for a fact that Haasini's parents would never agree to a marriage between the two. Why would they, when he didn't have a regular income even at the age of thirty-two? Nor did he have a family. The only thing he had to his credit was his good looks. And he had used it on Haasini without qualms.

Haasini wasn't complaining even now; not after failing in the relationship miserably. She had put down her time with Yeshwant to her life experience. Only after reaching his rented flat and staying there for a few days, had she realised that all Yeshwant had wanted, needed, was a free housekeeper. Who better than a wife? Only she had been too smart to marry the man.

That they had had sex didn't really bother her. After all, it was an itch she had had, a strong one at that. And he had helped her scratch it. What Haasini had realised in the process was that sex was overrated. It was no great shakes and orgasm was a complete myth. Once she came out of the stupor, she had taken her life into her hands and set about making plans to become independent. There was no way she was going to serve the mighty Yeshwant for the rest of her life. She had woken up to what he was, pretty early in their relationship. Not one to crib about the past, she had made concrete plans for the future and moved out of his apartment three months after she left Bengaluru.

She had moved into a homestay accommodation—a bedroom with an attached bath—in exchange for cooking breakfast, lunch, and dinner for the guests. She was truly grateful to her mother Jyothi, who had taught her to cook all kinds of food.

It was a convenient exchange in the beginning as both food and lodging were taken care off without spending a single rupee. As the number of guests increased, she began to get a salary in exchange for the time she spent in the kitchen. And she really enjoyed creating imaginative meals for the guests, whether four or forty, depending on how crowded the accommodation was on a given day. As for her free hours, she spent all of them working on her blog which was already a year old and had a good following.

Being a gregarious Cancerian by nature, Haasini spent her evenings with the guests as they played music, read books together or simply sat around chatting as they sipped on beer or wine. Haasini left a mark on everyone she met as she was warm and friendly. She even worked on her menus after consulting with the guests. It was a good thing the owner had given her a free hand after seeing her enthusiasm and her penchant for diligent work.

It wasn't long before Haasini made a lot of money with her well-honed writing skills. Being the crab that she was, she hoarded most of it in her bank account, grinning to herself every time she checked the increasing balance in it.

It was only yesterday when Haasini had felt a sudden urge to meet her parents. Her sister Janani wasn't so important. After all, she had never got along with her sibling who was four years older than her. But Haasini was fond of her parents, especially her mother. Not having taken even one day off in her twenty-two-month career as the cook at the homestay, Haasini had requested for a month's leave. The owner had been unable to refuse her.

Quickly packing her bags, Haasini had booked a train ticket to Bengaluru, not keen to think too much about her actions, as always.

But now, sitting idly as she munched through her breakfast, Haasini wondered about her parents' reaction. Will they let her into their house after the way she had sneaked out of it in the middle of the night, leaving only a brief note telling them that she was going away with Yeshwant Sharma and they shouldn't come searching for her? She had even pointed out that she was over eighteen and they didn't have a right to force her to go back home.

Tch!

Was it any surprise that she felt so old and wise a couple of years later?!

vantika was sitting in the plane which was leaving for Bengaluru when her phone rang. "Vidu! So glad you called. What happened to you and Janani? *Appa*...?"

"The very reason I called you, Avi," said Vidyut in a frustrated voice. "Do the parents know the time of your flight?"

Avantika didn't have to think before answering. "Not really. They know I'm landing in Bengaluru today, that's it."

"Good. I'll pick you up. We need to talk."

Her face broke out in an affectionate smile. She adored her brother who was older than her by three years. "Can't wait." It had been some months since they chatted together face-to-face. Seeing the air hostess waving in her direction, Avantika said, "I need to switch off my phone. My flight's taking off."

"See you soon."

Vidyut was waiting at the Kempegowda International Airport, Bengaluru when Avantika stepped out with her single trolley bag, looking stylish in dark blue designer jeans and a full-sleeved t-shirt in the palest of pink. Her hair was tied up in a high ponytail while her brown eyes shone with excitement when she caught sight of her tall brother. "Vidu," she flew into his arms as he enfolded her in a bear hug.

"Avi! It's so good to see you. I can see that marriage to Shatru suits you well."

Avantika grinned, nodding vigorously. "Shatru suits me really well, marriage or no marriage," she responded cheekily, tucking her hand in the crook of his elbow as they walked to the car park. "Where are we going?" she asked, pulling the seatbelt in place.

"To Kamath's Koffee. I want to talk to you before *Appa* and *Amma* get there."

Avantika gave him a shrewd look. "They were twisting your arm to get married to Janani, right? I thought so!" She snapped her fingers, a scowl on her neat forehead.

Vidyut grimaced. "Smart as ever. *Appa* didn't give me a chance to say no when he threw a lot of logical arguments at me. Which is exactly the reason I insisted on a long engagement."

"You mean you hoped to break it off at some point?" Avantika shook her head. "That's so not you, Vidu. You are way more straightforward than that." It just wasn't his style to be sneaky. If he had committed to marry Janani, Vidyut would have definitely married her, even if it killed him.

"Thanks." Vidyut reached across to squeeze her hand. "At least you know me well, sis." He sighed. "*Appa's* going ballistic that I am not going to marry Janani. But it wasn't I who broke off the engagement."

Avantika stared at him, a confused scowl on her face. "Don't tell me she was the one who called it off!

But why would Janani do that? She seemed keen on an arranged match and from what I understood, she wasn't too much into building a career or any such thing. Her main aim in life was to get married and settle down with a family of her own." She was glad to be able to voice her opinion freely now that Vidyut was no longer betrothed to the woman. Avantika hadn't believed Janani was the right partner for her brother, not by a long shot. But then, she had felt it wasn't fair to interfere.

Vidyut gave his sister a strange look. To be truthful, he hadn't really considered Janani's motives in agreeing to marry him. And they never seemed to find the right opportunity to get to know each other, not in six months. She was too busy to meet him whenever he was free. And the few times they got together, she had kept her distance, both physically and mentally. The worst part was that he hadn't really cared.

"Let me be truthful, Avi. While it was she who returned the ring, I am totally relieved that we aren't going to get married. Do you think I'm being wicked?" he asked, lifting an eyebrow at her as he slid the car into the parking slot allotted to him in the compound where his coffee shop was set.

Avantika turned to look at Vidyut, surprise on her face. But she burst out laughing when she caught the dancing mischief in his brown gaze, the exact shade as her own. "Vidu! You are extremely wicked, that's what you are," she declared, laughing some more.

They walked into Kamath's Koffee, the place almost ready with only a couple of workers giving the finishing touches before the grand opening two days later.

Avantika stopped in the middle, turning around in a circle as she eyed the café, her keen eyes not missing anything. "This is so incredible!" she said in an awed whisper when she finally stopped in front of him. "You have truly given life to your dream, Vidu."

He grinned at her, throwing an arm around her shoulders. "Haven't I?!" He sighed. "It's just that *Appa* is so damn unhappy. And *Amma* does whatever he tells her like the obedient wife she is."

"Neither of them has visited this place?"

He shook his head, his mouth drooping at the corners. "Nope."

"But you bought the property two months back and have been working on it from the beginning. What's wrong with them?" Avantika was angry on her brother's behalf.

"Stubborn! That's what *Appa* is. You must remember what happened when he heard of Shatru's lifestyle for the first time."

"*Appa* was so angry," Avantika laughed. "And he was astounded when I listed the varied careers all his brothers had."

"It took a lot of persuading, but he came around."

"True." She hooked her arm into his. "It was all thanks to you. You are the best brother in the world."

"Thanks, sis, but not really. He would have been a fool to refuse Shatru. Your husband is a gem of a man and *Appa* knows that only too well now."

Colour ran up Avantika's face as she heard Vidyut's praise for her husband, Shatrughan. She couldn't agree more. In the past year of being married to him, she had only fallen more in love with her bohemian husband who's thirst for wanderlust still ruled supreme. Not that she minded, as nowadays Avantika got to travel with Shatrughan to whichever part of the globe he was visiting; and in style too. But when her father, Arun Kamath, heard of Shatrughan and his penchant for globetrotting, he had refused to agree to Avantika marrying a man who had no permanent job or regular salary. It had taken a lot of patience and persuasion on Vidyut's part to convince their father to at least meet Shatrughan and get to know him before refusing the alliance. The rest was history as Arun and Vandana had been only too impressed with Shatrughan and the Maheshwari family who were based in Jaipur. And that was when they finally gave their blessings to the match between Avantika and her husband.

"Forget Janani! Don't you like any other girl, Vidyut? Isn't there anyone you want to be your life partner?" she asked her brother seriously. She could understand where the parents were coming from. After all, Vidyut was thirty and it was time he had a partner. Though she wasn't one to tell him he should marry the first girl who came along. Which seemed to have been the case with Janani Rai.

Vidyut shrugged. "Not really." He had had a couple of affairs when he was in the US. But there was no one he felt attracted to, not after returning home to Bengaluru.

"What about Janani? It wasn't nice of her to return the ring. But why didn't you even try to get her back?" He had been roguish that way, thought Avantika.

Vidyut couldn't help grinning as he walked with her behind the counters to the kitchen, preparing coffee while she checked out the latest gadgets as she circled the area. "Didn't I mention to a feeling of relief when she returned my ring?" he asked, pouring coffee into two white mugs that had the café's logo on one side and an eye-roll emoji in sunny yellow on the other.

"Very funny, Vidu. What would have happened if she hadn't? Would you have married her in January as you were all planning?" she asked, giving him a stern look as she took a mug from him and checking out the logo which was a stylish pattern of KK entwined. "I like this logo. Your design?"

He tilted his head before replying to her first question. "Now that you mention it, it's not funny, not at all." He gave a shudder. "I realise it now that I am free of the match. And I don't even want to think about what might have happened in January. Damn it, Avi! What can I say? I don't think Janani was interested in me as a person. It was what I represented. A great job that brought in a steady salary month after month; security; whatever."

"Don't be an idiot, Vidu. You're short selling yourself. Come on, you aren't just the job you do. You look handsome, you value your family, you are creating a stunning brand with your coffee shop, you are also a number of other things. You…"

"You know all that. But Janani…" he grimaced, shaking his head, "she knows nothing about me. At least, not the real me that matters."

"How much do *you* know about her?" asked Avantika, perching on one of the kitchen counters as she sipped her coffee.

"She looks beautiful… hmm… let me see… like a mannequin. You know something, Avi, I've never seen her smile, not once." He sounded amazed as if he had made a new discovery right that very minute. "She teaches children in the first grade. Shouldn't a primary teacher exude more warmth?" he asked.

"I want to shake you up," growled Avantika angrily, keeping her half full mug down with a thud and shaking her fists at him. "Why the hell did you agree to the match in the first place?"

Vidyut placed his empty mug aside as he ran his hand over the back of his head, appearing confounded. "I don't really know. *Appa* went on and on about my being thirty and how it was time I settled down. I really didn't have time for a non-existent girlfriend as my job was taking up sixty hours in a week. I was simply hating it and my mind was numb, I think. That's when he set the ball rolling to find me a suitable match. He caught hold of me one Sunday morning and dragged me over to meet Janani and her family. Everything kind of steamrollered from that point. There was really no reason for me to say no. I wasn't in love with any other girl. And Janani was completely eligible in the parents' eyes. And…" he shrugged, "I became engaged, just like that."

Avantika had flown down for the engagement in the afternoon and left the same night as she was travelling to Boston the very next day to join Shatrughan for a stint in America. Neither Avantika nor Vidyut had had an opportunity to talk about his engagement and the woman he had been going to marry. "I think the only smart thing you did at that point was to insist on a year's worth of engagement," said Avantika.

He threw back his head and laughed. "Tell me about it. It must be my Destiny speaking to me from within.

It must have known that the engagement wouldn't last until then."

Avantika couldn't help laughing as she jumped off the counter to punch him on his arm with a tight fist. "You are incorrigible, Vidu. No wonder *Appa* is angry. How do you plan to pacify him?" she asked. "If you as the "son" of the family," she drew quotation marks in the air, "is unable to calm him down, what can I, a mere female, do?"

"Bullshit!" he said, taking her hand and walking up the stairs to the first floor. "You are the favourite child nowadays; married to the wonderful Shatrughan Maheshwari and travelling to exotic places. Unlike I, who has quit a lucrative job and also let go of the only woman who ever showed interest in marrying me," said Vidyut cheekily.

"Shut up, Vidu! I can't stop laughing," stammered Avantika, as bubbles of laughter burst forth from within her. "She's the only woman who showed interest in marrying you? That's bullshit, if you ask me. Shall I take out an advertisement in the matchmaking column of some newspaper? Do you want to find out how many women queue up to meet you?"

"You mean I don't have enough problems on my plate now?" asked Vidyut, trying to bring a puppy dog expression to his face and failing miserably.

It only made Avantika laugh all the more.

Vidyut walked around his café, stopping to chat with his guests—a hundred of them invited while the rest were strangers who had been lured by gift coupons which he had had distributed over the past week—the coupon getting them a twenty-five percent discount on a beverage and a snack.

While thrilled at the crowd and the quickly disappearing refreshments, his gaze kept going back to the five-tiered cake which had been set up in the middle of the restaurant on a square table, one of the hired students keeping guard over it.

Avantika walked towards Vidyut to hook her arm around his, giving him a wide smile. "This place is incredible, Vidu. I am so, so proud of you." She went on tiptoe to kiss his lean cheek.

His answering smile not quite reaching his eyes, Vidyut asked her, "Any news?"

She gave a small shake of her head before turning towards the customers and smiling at them in greeting.

All the invitees were here and were eagerly waiting for Vidyut to cut the cake. But their parents—Arun and Vandana Kamath—were conspicuously absent. Many of the older relatives had already asked them both when Arun and Vandana would make an appearance.

His father, Arun Kamath, was extremely cut up with Vidyut. The first reason was that Vidyut had given up his plush job to start his own business, Kamath's Koffee. The second was that his engagement had been called off, through no fault of his.

So angry was Arun that he had refused to come for the inauguration of Kamath's Koffee; while also stopping his wife Vandana from attending it.

Quickly realising that things were not how they should be, Shatrughan offered to go to his brother-in-law's rescue. Avantika's husband of fourteen months, Shatrughan Maheshwari understood family and relationships only too well. "You leave Uncle and Aunty to me, Vidu; and take care of your guests. Avantika will keep you company. Let me go bring your parents." He walked out of the café after giving Vidyut a quick hug, determined to persuade his parents-in-law to attend their son's café inauguration.

Ringing the bell, Shatrughan didn't have to wait long before Vandana opened the door to their bungalow. "Welcome, welcome *aliya*," she invited her son-in-law—addressing him formally in Kannada, the local language—with a smile which didn't quite reach her anxious eyes. "Are you coming from the airport?" Avantika hadn't mentioned anything about her husband coming over for Kamath's Koffee's opening.

Shatrughan walked into the Kamaths' home, bending down to touch his mother-in-law's feet. "I had gone to Vidyut's café directly from the airport. When I saw that you and uncle weren't there, I offered to take you both back with me." His expression firm, he asked, "Where's Arun Uncle?"

"Shatrughan, welcome. How have you been?" Arun stepped out of his room to shake his son-in-law's hand, giving him a wary glance.

"I'm good, Uncle. But why aren't you ready yet? The guests are all already assembled at the café."

Shatrughan had arrived only that afternoon and had gone directly to Kamath's Koffee, Avantika having arrived a couple of days earlier to lend her support to her brother.

Arun took a deep breath, wondering how to deal with the situation without antagonising his daughter's husband. "Er…"

"Uncle!" Shatrughan placed a pacifying hand on the older man's shoulder. "I understand that you are upset with Vidyut for a number of reasons. But we can deal with all that in private. We don't want to wash our dirty linen in public, do we? After all, we are one family. Isn't it what you parents have taught us?" He turned to include Vandana in the conversation. "You cannot let down your son like this, Uncle."

"You don't know what all he has done, *aliya*. I agree Vidyut is my son. But he's all grown up now and he doesn't listen to me anymore," said Arun bitterly, going to sit on the sofa. "Vandana, why don't you give Shatrughan some coffee? I will also have some."

Vandana stood there, reluctant to move away from the living room, a spark of hope in her eyes. The mother so wanted to go to the inauguration of her son's café.

"Wait, Aunty. I don't want to have coffee just now. You shouldn't either, Uncle. Let's go and try out the variety of blends which Vidyut has put together. Listen, Uncle. I can understand that you are upset for various things. But this is a proud moment. Your son is beginning something new and he needs your blessings." He put both his palms together in a pleading gesture. "Please get ready and come with me, Uncle, for my sake."

Arun jumped up from the sofa to prise Shatrughan's hands apart. After all, how could he let his son-in-law plead with him? "No, no. Please, *aliya*, you should not plead with us. I will go with you, only because you are asking me to, do you understand?"

Shatrughan nodded, biting his lip to stop the smile of triumph which tried to break out on his face. "Get ready fast, then. The guests are all waiting for you both."

Vandana dashed a hand over her teary eyes before giving her son-in-law a grateful glance. "Just five minutes."

"Huh! She will take at least half an hour," said Arun challengingly as he walked towards his room. "I'll be ready way before that."

It was Vandana who stepped out of their room first. She had just had to change into the Mysore silk saree as she had already worn the new silk blouse and matching petticoat way before Shatrughan had arrived to pick them up; as she had hoped against hope that somehow, she would be able to attend the function.

"I am glad you came, *aliya*," she told him gratefully.

"You should have known that if it wasn't me, then Vidyut would have himself come for you both. How can he begin his new venture without his parents by his side?" Shatrughan hugged the half-tearful Vandana.

"Try telling your stubborn father-in-law that," sniffed Vandana with a grimace.

He laughed. "Don't be upset, Aunty. Uncle will come around."

"I heard that," said Arun, stepping out, clothed in a three-piece suit which Vidyut had insisted on buying for him, just for the occasion. "Let me tell you upfront, Shatrughan. I don't plan to forgive Vidyut easily."

Shatrughan gave his father-in-law a solemn nod as they stepped out of the house before Arun locked it behind them. He had driven over in Vidyut's car. Once the parents settled in, Shatrughan got into the driver's seat and drove swiftly and steadily over to Kamath's Koffee.

"Is there a big crowd?" asked Arun, curious despite himself.

"At least eight hundred people, Uncle," said Shatrughan, smiling at Avantika's father.

"Oh!" Arun was truly impressed, though he didn't plan to admit to it.

Vandana had no such qualms. "Eight hundred! That's a lot of people. It must be a gala affair."

"It is, Aunty. There's even a huge cake to be cut. Vidyut refused to cut it without the two of you next to him."

"He's my son. I didn't expect anything less of him." Vandana muttered in an undertone, looking at her husband from the corner of her eyes.

"I didn't expect a lot of things which your son did. What about all those?" Arun turned around to growl at her.

"Uncle!" Shatrughan laid a pacifying hand on his father-in-law's arm, "Shall we talk about all that later?

After we return from the inauguration? I promise to take your side."

"Thanks, *aliya*. You are truly a gem." Arun calmed down immediately, only to please his son-in-law. As for his son, he planned to let both Avantika and Shatrughan deal with Vidyut.

Avantika checked her phone when it pinged. "On way with parents," was Shatrughan's message.

"Vidu, they should be here soon. Both *Appa* and *Amma* are coming over with Shatru."

"Phew!" Vidyut gave her a weak grin before throwing his arms around his sister and hugging her close. "Shatru is truly a heaven send. Remind me to thank him properly."

Avantika laughed, feeling so proud of both her husband and her brother. "He's the best! And so are you!"

Vandana got out the moment Shatrughan stopped the car in front of the entrance to Kamath's Koffee, lifting her face to check out the fairy lights twinkling all the way from the first floor down to the ground. She felt so thrilled to see the name board which was in bright red letters, pretty eye catching. And the crowd! Oh my God! The place was filled to more than overflowing if such a thing was possible.

"Come along, Aunty." Shatrughan took her hand, his other hand holding Arun's and walked into the café with the two of them.

Vidyut rushed to the entrance when he caught sight of his brother-in-law with his parents' hands firmly held in his. "*Appa, Amma!*" He bent down to touch their feet in turn before hugging Shatrughan.

"Thank you, bro!" he whispered, his voice breaking with emotion.

"Don't be so formal, Vidu. Come now, let's go cut the cake."

Arun and Vandana took their time walking to the centre table as many relatives and friends stopped them to offer their good wishes, telling them how lucky they were to have a son like Vidyut.

Surprised at their words, but unable to stop the spark of pride as he glanced over the large space with shining counters, thronged by excited guests, Arun thanked everyone, shaking their hands even as he walked as quickly as possible to the table holding the tall cake.

Vidyut pointed to the knife which had a red ribbon tied in a smart bow around its handle. "*Amma, Appa,* you both must cut the cake together," he said, his dark eyes shining with happiness.

Vandana took the knife and stood next to her husband before insisting, "Vidu, Avi, *aliya,* come! Let's all of us cut the cake together."

Arun gave a nod, unable to stop the smile which stretched his lips. He had expected a cubbyhole all because his son had told him that he had purchased the property. He just couldn't believe his eyes when he saw how big the place was. At least fifteen hundred square feet. And there was a first floor besides this as well. Amazing! Shatrughan had mentioned that there were eight hundred guests. Though it seemed crowded, the space seemed enough for so many people. He hadn't missed noticing a lot of people who were standing on the staircase, their phone cameras trained on the Kamath family. Holding his wife's hand along with the others, he cut the cake, emotion choking his vocal cords when a loud applause broke out from all around them.

Champagne flutes were raised by the invitees as they toasted Vidyut and Kamath's Koffee before Vidyut fed pieces of cake to all members of his family. Avantika quickly sliced the cake and placed the pieces on trays which the employees carried around the room, offering to all those present.

The crowd that had made it to the restaurant along with discount coupons were thrilled to get a taste of the chocolate cake which was on the house and each man and woman as one swore to return to the coffee shop at an earliest possible date.

"You worked a miracle there, bro," said Vidyut, raising his champagne flute to clink it with Shatrughan's.

Shatrughan laughed. "It was to be expected. Am I not their *aliya*? The special son-in-law as your parents call me in your mother tongue? They couldn't very well say no to me, could they?"

Vidyut threw back his head and laughed heartily, turning the heads of many of the young female guests, not that he was aware of it.

It was way past ten when the last guests left, congratulating the family once again on their way out.

Vidyut thanked all his employees for the excellent job they had done and locked the place up for the night. Kamath's Koffee was ready to run its business from the day after tomorrow.

5

H aasini Rai was frazzled when she stepped into Kamath's Koffee, folding her wet umbrella before placing it in the plastic bucket provided for it at the entrance. It was pouring cats and dogs in Bengaluru, making her feel chilled to the bone. She took a deep whiff of the aroma of freshly brewed coffee, a small smile lighting up her narrow face. Aah! Coffee! Her favourite beverage.

Looking around the crowded restaurant, she saw an empty table for two in the furthest corner on the left side and quickly walked over to place her laptop bag on one of the chairs. Perfect! No one would disturb her in this corner. Turning, she walked to the counter even as she checked the handwritten menus at the back.

"One Mocha Latte, large…" she looked down to see what was available in the display cabinets before continuing, "…one veg quiche and a slice of blueberry cheesecake."

"Sure, ma'am," said the girl at the counter, "That'll be Rs 698. Cash or card?"

"Card." Haasini pulled out her debit card from her wallet and handed it over.

The transaction was completed and the girl gave her the bill and a plastic tab to mark her table for the waiter to find her. "Table 27. Your order will be delivered in five minutes, ma'am."

"Thanks." Haasini started back to the corner table, her lips drooping once again, unaware of the male gazes following her slender figure clad in dark tan capris and white t-shirt as she walked.

Today had been one of the worst mornings of her life. Haasini shook her head to herself as she recalled the endless arguments with her mother while her father gave her the silent treatment. And to think she had arrived home only last week, that too after two years. Sigh!

Prodigal daughter! That was what she was. But her parents hadn't welcomed her with open arms, more like a grimace actually. Nor had they brought out the best wine or killed a fatted calf for her sake. No, not at all!

Haresh and Jyothi had been wearing an expression like, "What the hell are you doing here?"

Shit! Dumping the glass of water she had been carrying, Haasini grabbed a couple of tissues from the elegant ceramic container on the table and dabbed at her capri pants where she had spilled water because of her trembling hand. *Can't I get a damn thing right?!*

She removed her laptop from her bag; sitting down on the chair and booting it before plugging it into the electrical outlet next to her table. The coffee shop even offered free internet for all customers ordering food worth a minimum of two hundred and fifty bucks. Not bad at all!

Kamath's Koffee was two weeks old and already the public were talking about it a lot. The reviews on

Zomato and Trip Advisor were all four and five stars for the food as well as the ambience. Sipping water, Haasini studied the area in front of her. The place was fully packed with maybe one or two empty tables. Then again, some of the tables for six had more people sitting around as college students had dragged chairs over to the table to better be able to hang out with their friends. Waiters, youngsters who were probably also students, went from one table to another with the customers' orders.

To her knowledge, the coffee shop was situated on the ground and first floors, with a seating capacity of one hundred people on each level.

It was true that Kamath's Koffee was situated next to two colleges and multiple offices in the heart of the city; and hence the crowd on a weekday morning.

Haasini thanked the waiter who brought her order and placed the tray on the table. "Thank you, Nirmal," she said, smiling at the young man even as she read his name on the tag. "Tell me something. Who is the owner of this place?"

"Mr Vidyut Kamath, ma'am," said Nirmal.

Taking a sip of her chocolate flavoured coffee, she asked, "Is he on the premises? I was wondering if I could meet him."

"I can find out, ma'am. This would be regarding…?"

"I write for a newspaper and I'm keen to know more about this coffee shop. It's new, isn't it?" she asked, forking a piece of the blueberry cheese cake into her mouth. She automatically closed her eyes as she savoured the melt-in-the-mouth taste, not noticing the smile on Nirmal's face.

Not really surprised by her reaction to the dessert, Nirmal said, "It's sixteen days old, ma'am. Let me find out if Vidyut sir is free."

"You do that. And my compliments to the chef. The cake is simply fabulous."

"I'll pass on your message, ma'am." *Or you can do it yourself if he's free to meet you,* thought Nirmal to himself as he did an about turn and walked behind the counter where the kitchen was.

The veg quiche was even better than the cake. Cynically wondering if it was all because it was new—something like new brooms sweeping clean and all that—Haasini put down her first impressions in a Word document on her laptop. She wondered if she would need permission to take pictures on her phone. It was ten minutes since Nirmal, the waiter, had gone to find out if his boss would meet her, but there was no news so far.

Anyway, she had the whole day to herself. Reviewing films and restaurants was Haasini's passion and she had made a name for herself by building her blog. There were a number of newspapers and a couple of TV channels she freelanced for after her blog became extremely popular. Money was there; way more than what she needed. It was love that was lost to her.

At twenty, she had eloped with Yeshwant Sharma, believing the man when he told her that he loved her more than his life. His promise of marriage didn't have a chance to materialise as it wasn't long before Haasini realised that he had wanted someone to do the cooking and cleaning at his apartment in Mysuru for free. She had left him after three months. Not keen to return home to face her parents' wrath, Haasini had moved into a homestay in Mysuru; taking up the job of cooking for the guests. It was while working there that she had set up her blog, soon learning all the tricks which helped her earn an income. It hadn't been long before she started freelancing for mainstream media and making a hell of a lot of money, way more than she had imagined.

It was pride which had kept her away from returning to her parents' home for two whole years. And then there was her sister, Janani. Janani was the apple of her parents' eye; the good girl who always toed the line, unlike Haasini, who was the very bane of their existence.

Tch!

Haasini rubbed a hand on her forehead, her eyes shut as she willed the nagging headache to go away, when she sensed someone standing next to her. Opening her eyes, she looked up, and up some more before her dark gaze clashed with brown eyes. The man was standing too damn close, into her space. With a deep frown pleating her forehead, she glared at him, sure that he would move away when he noticed her angry expression.

Only he didn't. "Hello," said he, offering his hand, "I'm Vidyut Kamath. I was told you wanted to meet me."

Her frown cleared immediately to be replaced with a smile, as Haasini finally noticed the apron he wore, the chef's cap thrust carelessly into the pocket at the front. "Hello Vidyut. I am Haasini." She placed her small hand in his large one, feeling a sudden tug at her heart as it clamoured against her ribcage, trying to jump into her throat. She quickly withdrew her hand and pointed to the empty chair in front of her, saying, "Why don't you sit down?" in a croaky voice.

"Sure." Vidyut sat down to study the young woman in front of him, wondering if he had seen her before. There was something familiar about her features. Mentally shaking his head after a couple of moments, he decided that he had never seen her or he wouldn't have forgotten. She had a narrow face with a pointed chin, her large and dark eyes with their ever-so-long lashes her most striking feature. She looked cute and was probably a student. "Did you enjoy your order, Haasini?" he asked, giving her a smile which made her sit up and take notice.

He was a walking, talking temptation! Strikingly handsome with voluminous, straight hair which was cut short, a broad forehead, thick shapely eyebrows and an aquiline nose, Vidyut Kamath was pure tantalisation. The slashing cheeks were free of fuzz while the sculpted lips oozed raw sensuality. His eyes were a golden brown, reminding her of melting chocolate, with heavy lids and thick, short eyelashes. And then there were the dimples which formed when he smiled.

Dishy! That was what he was.

Suddenly realising that he was waiting for her answer, she said, "You seem to have an excellent baker on board. And the chocolate coffee blend is to die for."

Ruddy colour washed over Vidyut's face when he heard her wholesome compliment. To his knowledge, news reporters rarely said anything praiseworthy, at least not to someone's face. He had read articles peppered with sarcasm more than anything else when the newspapers reviewed restaurants. He was surprised and pleased with Haasini's comments. "Nirmal says you write for a newspaper…?" Vidyut lifted his eyebrow at her.

"That's right. I am a freelancer, actually. I have a blog called *Coffee Pe Charcha*. I…"

"You are *that* Haasini! Haasini Rai, who's a connoisseur of restaurants. I don't believe it!" Vidyut was grinning from ear to ear, truly unable to believe his luck. This slight young woman was the blogger the restaurateurs revered. One post on her blog, even with a three or a four-star rating, was considered a great honour, giving a tremendous boost to one's business.

Finding his grin infectious, Haasini returned it with equal merit. She was always surprised when someone recognised her name or her blog, even after three years; the success having never gone to the Cancer woman's head.

"May I have your bill, Haasini? I will ensure that the money is returned to you immediately," Vidyut offered.

Haasini shook her head. "Thank you, but no, Vidyut. I pay my own way. It helps me give people honest feedback. I'm sure you know what I mean."

He nodded slowly, saying, "Fair enough."

"So, who's your baker?" she asked, typing furiously into her laptop.

Curious to know what she was working on in such a hurry, Vidyut replied, "I am."

She stopped typing to look up at him, her mouth falling open. This hunk was a chef?! How incredible was that! "I thought you were the owner."

"You thought right."

"You are also the chef?" She shook her head as if to clear it.

"Not "the chef"," he said, drawing quotation marks in the air. "I handle the coffee blends—a favourite part of my job, I should say; and do the baking. There are two other chefs who take care of the rest of the menu."

She closed the lid of her laptop to sit back and concentrate on him completely, just in case she missed something important. "Let me get this correct. You are the creator of the amazing Mocha Latte, the veg quiche and the blueberry cheesecake I had today?" She felt her heart thumping in excitement. It was so damn impressive that such an attractive man could cook so deliciously as well.

"That's me." Vidyut bowed his head, a mite startled at the heat rising in his cheeks, her praise going to his head like rum on an empty stomach.

"What do the other chefs do?" she asked, opening her laptop once again. She had seen the hand-written menu behind the counter. That had contained only the highlights, not the whole variety.

"Why Haasini? We have a four-page menu worth of dishes. We serve typical South Indian delicacies like *idli, dosa, upma* and *vada*; regular ones, and also those with a twist; something like a fusion cuisine. And we also have rice items like *bisi bele bath, puliyodharai*, etcetera. We also serve fresh fruit juices, only seasonal ones."

"That's a lot of stuff for a coffee shop, wouldn't you say?" Haasini continued to type as she asked him the questions. "Are there takers for the rice items?"

"Even I was surprised at the demand," admitted Vidyut.

"Do you do home delivery?"

"No, we don't."

"Any plans to tie up with Swiggy or Zomato?" she asked.

Vidyut took a deep breath before saying, "Nothing so far. We are just managing to keep ahead of the walk-in crowd. Maybe sometime in the future. Right now, I am keen that people come here and get a feel of the ambience."

"Oh yes, the ambience. Did you hire an interior decorator for this place?" She gave a swift glance around the area, the cheerful blinds pulled partway down the floor-length windows; the posters on the side walls, the well-polished counters displaying trays filled with the different items which were served. She looked at the staircase on one side which went up to the first floor.

Seeing her glancing around, Vidyut asked, "Would you like a tour of the first floor?"

"That would be nice." Haasini got up to walk up to the first floor with him, her gaze going to his tight butt as he took the stairs, a shiver running down her spine. She had never felt such a strong attraction to any man in her life. Even Yeshwant had been a means to an end is what she had realised some months after she left him. "Do you have partners?" she asked.

"Nope. I am solo," he said, turning to glance down at her.

The first floor was more than half full. In one corner were ice-cream dispensing machines, manned by a student.

"You have students working for you."

He smiled. "Yes, I find they are the most enthusiastic."

"What happens during exams?"

"Not everyone has exams at the same time, do they? I'll work out a timetable." He had it all planned out. He knew how important pocket money was to students, especially those who were not native to Bengaluru. While he had told his mother he had six students working for him, what he meant was he had three batches of six students, each working four-hour shifts. It was working really well so far.

Vidyut insisted on getting her a butterscotch ice-cream cone when she mentioned it was her favourite.

"Don't think this is going to earn your coffee shop any brownie points," she said, licking her way through the large scoop of the delicious cold dessert.

"The last I heard, even being given a negative rating on your blog brings notice to restaurants," he laughed. "But tell me, is that true?"

"You're kidding me. First of all, I've never given a negative rating on my blog. Secondly, who will go to a restaurant with bad rating?" She shook her head at him before walking down the staircase. Seeing him checking his phone, she asked, "Do you have time for a few more questions? Or do you need to get back to your oven? I should have probably taken an appointment. I…"

"No issues, Haasini. I have the time. I just received a message from the kitchen that they are managing very well without me getting underfoot." He laughed. "Talking of which, you are welcome to a tour of our kitchen."

"That would be great. Will it be alright if I take pictures?"

"Most definitely. Do you use a camera?"

"My phone. Oneplus 7T has an excellent camera."

He nodded. "Come along then."

6

Haasini let herself into her home—truthfully, her parents' home, as she didn't feel really welcome—at nine that night. She had completed the article and sent it along with select pictures to the daily, Bengaluru Express, to be published in their Friday edition. As for an article on her blog, she planned to publish a different angle; like the interview with Vidyut. She might have to meet him a couple of more times to gather enough information.

The man was interesting, most definitely. No, she wasn't going to think about the way her heart had leapt into her throat when she shook his hand. He had patiently taken her on a tour of his pristine kitchen, introducing her to the other two chefs. She clicked a lot of pictures of the whole place; some with the staff and she had even posed in a few which Vidyut offered to click for her. With a reminiscent smile on her face, Haasini quickly walked across to a veranda off the living room and placed her open umbrella there so that it could dry out.

She stopped in her tracks when she heard voices in the dining hall. Should she join her family for dinner? She wasn't really hungry. But then, she had to meet them some time, didn't she? Changing direction, she went into the narrow room between the living room and the kitchen and felt a tug of envy when she saw her parents and sister looking cosy as they ate their meal together.

"Hello everyone!" Her voice was gruff with emotion as she walked towards them to pull a chair out and sit down. Picking the glass of water next to her mother's plate, she drank from it. "What's for dinner?"

Haresh Rai scowled at his younger daughter, not having forgiven her for running away from home two years ago. What a shame it had been! He had become a laughing stock amongst his relatives and friends.

"Bangda fish curry and pulao," said Jyothi, eyeing her daughter without a smile. It hurt to smile whenever she thought of Haasini, the child she had loved with all her heart. The past two years hadn't been easy, her husband's anger yielding no mercy. Jyothi had borne the brunt of his temper as he heaped abuse on his wife for bringing up their daughter so badly. Even now, despite all the irritation, Jyothi couldn't help the feeling of affection which tugged at her heart whenever she looked into her younger child's thin face. Haasini had lost a lot of weight. At twenty, she used to have a chubby face with her body leaning towards plumpness. Now she was not even lean, but thin; as if she had been starved. Or that's how it seemed to the mother.

"Janani, will you pass me a plate?" Haasini turned to her sister.

Janani handed a melamine plate to her younger sister without uttering a word; with no expression on her face. The fact was that Janani hated Haasini, who was younger to her by four years. Until she was born,

Janani had been the apple of her parents' eye. The four-year-old hadn't liked the new baby who had arrived to take the parents' attention away from her. Janani had never got along with her ambitious younger sister who had always wanted to make something of herself. For Janani, it was too much of an effort. She had ended up being a graduate, all because it was expected of her. Now, she taught first standard students at a local school, only because it helped her pass the time until she married a rich man and had a family of her own.

Vidyut Kamath had seemed like the perfect catch when her parents had discovered him through some friends. Educated in the USA and working for a multinational, he seemed to be an ideal choice. That he was also good-looking was a plus point. They had met the first time when Vidyut visited the Rais' home along with his parents. Having no reason to reject the alliance, Janani had fallen in with her parents' wishes and agreed to marry him. She had met Vidyut alone on only three occasions after that. The first two when they had met in coffee shops to chat briefly over the weekend. Remembering the note of warning from her parents, Janani had ensured that they never even held hands during those meetings.

And hadn't that been a good thing? She had felt betrayed when he changed his career overnight to open a coffee shop without even speaking to her about it. It never struck Janani that she had never given her fiancé an opportunity to speak about anything other than superficial topics. In fact, both the times they met, they had drunk their coffee in silence as they didn't have any common topic of interest to discuss.

Her father, Haresh Rai, had been angry and insulted when he found out about Vidyut's coffee shop. He had called Janani privately and spoken to her at length. "Look here, my dear. You sister is dead to me and you are my only child now. I want you to have a happy life. I really did my best to find you an excellent match. And believe me, Vidyut was that when we met him six months back. But I don't really understand this need he has to run a business of his own. He's young and quite immature for all we know. You should go and speak with him. Convince him that it's really important that he shouldn't give up his job. Can you do that?"

"Yes, Dad." Janani's heart was dancing with glee when she heard her father utter that her sister—Haasini— was dead to him. Served her right, the bitch! After all, hadn't Haasini dared to take away her parents' attention from Janani just by walking this earth?

"You have to be careful not to antagonise him, do you understand? You don't want to break the engagement, but to give Vidyut a word of warning. Make sure he listens to your advice."

"I understand, Dad. I will go tomorrow itself."

She had met Vidyut the next morning at his coffee shop. It had looked grand and all that. But what was the use? Her father knew for a fact that he was bound to fail. After all, it wasn't easy to run a restaurant in a city like Bengaluru where there were simply too many eateries. She had told her fiancé upfront that he should get back to working with the MNC or she would break off the engagement. The idiot hadn't budged from his stand and she had as good as thrown the ring in his face.

Janani had been sure that her parents would applaud her behaviour. But it looked like there was no pleasing them. Her father had been appalled with the way things had turned out. Her mother had been in tears, accusing her of being a fool. Tch!

There had been some kind of back and forth between her parents and Vidyut's. But nothing had come of it. All because Vidyut had stuck to his guns and refused to listen to anyone. So much so, that Janani and her parents had reached the conclusion that they were better off without him in their lives.

But before they could breathe easy, Haasini had suddenly returned home last week. Janani was disgusted with her shameless sister! Imagine running away with a man, probably losing her virginity in the process, and returning home after two years, as if nothing had happened. How could she?

Janani hadn't spoken a word to her sister after her return. Not that they had shared a close relationship before that. Haasini was a chatterbox and tended to hog the limelight whenever she was around. The past two years had been lovely, without her younger sister around to overshadow her. Janani just hated the idea of her sister coming back to live with them. The only thing that made her happy was the way their father ignored Haasini. How she wished her mother would do the same!

"This is so delicious, Mom." Haasini smiled at her mother, eating the rice and curry with her hand, licking her fingers. The aroma of the food had made her stomach growl, suddenly making her realise that she had had nothing to eat after the quiche and cheesecake that morning; just drinking cups of coffee through the day.

Jyothi smiled, her eyes shimmering with unshed tears as she served some more curry on her younger one's plate. "You have become so thin, Haasini."

Haasini shrugged, grinning. "My body must have missed your cooking, Mom."

Janani grimaced, pushing her chair back noisily to get up with her empty plate in her hand. Turning the other way, she carried it to the kitchen sink and washed it, trying to shut out their voices, not at all keen to know about the love they shared.

Haresh sat back to look from his wife to his younger daughter, a scowl on his face. He had tried telling his wife that Haasini didn't belong in their home and should be sent straight back out. But Jyothi, who always listened to him, had simply refused to follow his instructions in this case. As it is, she was angry with him because of their elder daughter's broken engagement.

"You know how simple Janani is. Why did you send her to talk to Vidyut? Shouldn't *you* have spoken to either him or his father instead?" Jyothi had turned her accusing eyes on her husband when Janani came home after returning the engagement ring.

Haresh had hemmed and hawed, not really sure how to deal with the situation which was not at all to his liking. He thought he had been clear in his instructions to Janani, to only speak to Vidyut and not to break off the engagement. He couldn't look his wife in the eye when he said, "I thought that as they were going to be man and wife in a few months, he would listen to Janani. Then again, I never thought she would behave so precipitately and throw the ring in his face. You know how it is with young men nowadays. I don't think Vidyut would have liked it if I had put any kind of pressure through his father." He grimaced, feeling rather desperate about the situation.

Firstly, having no son to carry his name and legacy had really affected Haresh Rai.

Next, his younger daughter, the one he had adored, had eloped with a scoundrel from their neighbourhood. Yeshwant Sharma was a poor relative of their neighbours. Neither they nor Haresh and his wife had been aware that Haasini and Yeshwant had been seeing each other until they found the notes they had left in their respective homes. The shame of it had broken Haresh's heart.

And now this! Janani's broken engagement. He didn't really know what to tell his elder daughter. He had sent her over to speak to her fiancé, to convince him to give up this funny idea of a startup and return to his secure job; and specifically, not to break off the engagement. But the girl was an idiot for sure. Another thought seeped into his mind at that moment which he tried to push back forcibly, without any success: *my Haasini would have never dealt with the situation like this.*

He looked at his wife pathetically. "Looking back, I can see that I should have spoken to Arun Kamath about this. Because of your daughter's behaviour, I don't even have a leg to stand on. Now, they will only point out that Janani threw the ring in Vidyut's face. *Che!* How could she do this?"

"Forget it, Dad," said Janani flippantly. "What if Vidyut goes? A dozen others will come. We can always pick and choose."

Both the parents stared at her, similar expressions of horror on their faces. Was it so easy?

Haresh continued to sit at the dining table, not uttering a word as he let their voices—Jyothi's and Haasini's—wash over him. It had been so long since they had spent time as a family. How much ever he tried to hold on to his anger, he couldn't help the love gushing from his heart. After all, she was his flesh and blood. How could he continue to hate Haasini?

It was past eleven when Vidyut drove back home the same night. The café shut its doors to new customers at half past nine, with the last stragglers lingering for another hour. They were open from 10.30 am to 10.30 pm with the students rotating shifts while the three chefs took their breaks on and off, whenever possible. He smiled to himself, thinking that the coffee shop was taking as much time as his job had done. But then, the difference was that he loved being the boss of Kamath's Koffee; living his dream as he cooked up a storm as well as he ran the business end.

And maybe it was a good thing he was no longer engaged to Janani. He seriously didn't know why he had agreed to the match in the first place. But his parents had really badgered him to settle down as he had been twenty-nine going on thirty.

How much ever he had argued that that was no reason to tie the knot, his father had been insistent. Just now, Vidyut felt so free; free from the job he had hated and free of the fiancée he had felt nothing for.

Yes! Absolutely nothing! Janani had invoked no feelings of either love or lust in him. If she had kept herself away by not even letting him take her hand in his, he had been equally to blame as he hadn't felt the urge to hold her hand. There simply had been no chemistry.

Thinking of chemistry took his mind to the time he had spent with Haasini today. Vidyut grimaced. Haasini Rai was a kid, probably in her early twenties. But still, he couldn't stop himself from gazing at her tall and slender figure in those cotton capris and t-shirt. She was shapely for one thing, despite being thin. And then there was her face! While she wasn't striking in repose, her whole face came alive when she spoke. And how much she talked! He grinned as he drove at a steady pace, glad that there wasn't all that much traffic.

He shook his head as if to clear it. Vidyut really didn't believe their paths would cross again. While he sincerely hoped that his father wasn't going to try to arrange his marriage yet again any time soon.

There had been hell to pay after Janani returned his ring. He hadn't called his parents immediately as he had had a lot of work that day, ensuring that as much of the work as possible was completed as the coffee shop inauguration was inching closer. Too busy to dwell on his broken engagement, he had forgotten all about Janani's visit; only to return home after nine at night to face his furious father.

"What is this I hear, Vidu?" snarled Arun the moment Vidyut let himself into the house.

"About what, *Appa*?" asked Vidyut coolly, even as he walked across the hall to the staircase which would take him up to his room. He needed a shower after being around the carpenters all day.

"Don't pretend not to understand." His father was shouting by now, effectively stopping Vidyut from climbing the stairs.

"I am not pretending about anything, *Appa*. Can this wait? I urgently need a shower."

"You have your shower first, Vidu, and come down for dinner. We can talk then," said Vandana, trying to calm down the situation. But she couldn't stop the worry which brought her eyebrows together in a deep frown.

Vidyut took the stairs, two at a time, wondering what was bothering his parents before he recalled Janani's visit to the café. Ouch! He had forgotten all about it! He quickly had a shower before pulling on a pair of shorts and t-shirt before rushing down the stairs.

His parents were seated at the dining table waiting for him. When he pulled a chair to sit down, his father began to shout, "How could you break off your engagement to Janani? Don't you have better sense?"

Vidyut looked at his father with raised brows. "Who told you I broke off the engagement?" he asked coolly, serving the *akki roti* and *vegetable kurma* on his plate before beginning to eat. "Aren't you guys eating?" he asked his parents, looking at their empty plates.

A dazed Vandana placed the food on her husband's plate before serving herself, not saying a word even though her mind was in a turmoil. She never cared for arguments and she knew for a fact that her husband was spoiling for a fight. And Arun wasn't wrong, was he? It was not very nice of Vidyut to break off the engagement like this. After all, he had been betrothed to that Janani for more than six months. What will people say?

"What did you think? That we wouldn't get to know if you didn't tell us?" challenged Arun, not touching his food as he glared at his son.

Vidyut shrugged. "I don't know who told you what. But I did not break the engagement. It was Janani who pulled off her ring and gave it to me."

"What?" Arun gave his son a shocked glance, confident that Vidyut would never lie to his parents or anyone else for that matter. It just was not in his son's makeup.

"She came to the café today morning and told me to give up my business and get back to my job." He recalled the way she had given him an ultimatum, as good as saying, 'my way or the highway'. The problem was that it hadn't even made him angry, just indifferent; which said a lot about the lack of a relationship between them.

"I can't really blame her for that," said Arun sarcastically, beginning to eat from his plate.

"How can you say that, Arun? It's not right that Janani tried to threaten Vidyut. I don't like it," said Vandana, scowling at her husband. Well, Arun was clear that Vandana should respect him as the man of the house. Didn't the same rule apply to Janani and Vidyut?

Vidyut couldn't help smiling at his mother before he forced himself to appear serious when he turned to his father. "I don't really blame her either, *Appa*. But that's what happened. I did not break off the engagement. Is that what her father said?"

"Haresh Rai called soon after Janani went back home and told her parents that the engagement was broken off. And I presumed…"

"...that I had done it. *Appa*, you know I have way more respect for you than that. I would never do such a thing without talking to you about it first." Vidyut spoke in a pacifying voice, well aware that it was a double blow to his father that his son had resigned from his cushy job and started a business; and now the broken engagement.

"Like the way you resigned your job without discussing it with me first?" asked Arun sarcastically.

"That was something different, *Appa*. That was a personal decision. But it was you and *Amma* who arranged my marriage to Janani. I wouldn't break it off without consulting with you first."

"Aren't you upset about it?" asked his father, looking at his son curiously. Vidyut appeared as calm as ever.

Vidyut shrugged. "You want the truth? I don't really care. I wasn't keen on an arranged marriage. I would rather wait to meet someone I really liked. But you didn't give me a choice and that's why I agreed to it. But it's obvious that destiny has something entirely different planned for me."

"What nonsense are you talking about, Vidu? You are thirty and not really growing younger every day.

"So what?" Vidyut looked at his father earnestly. "I have a business to run, *Appa*. I really don't have the time for a wife in my life; or kids for that matter. Things were different when you were younger. You had a nine to five job and *Amma* was okay with being a housewife. Girls these days want careers too. Juggling a family and a rocking career isn't really easy. Why rush into it?"

Arun sighed exaggeratedly. "So, when do you plan to wed? When you are fifty?"

Vidyut laughed out loud. "Please, *Appa*. Why can't we live one day at a time? I will marry when I find the right woman, I promise."

"What if we don't like her?" asked Vandana in a worried voice. Did her son have a lover back in America? What if he brought home a foreigner? She grew anxious at the thought.

Vidyut laughed some more as he leaned across to kiss his mother on her cheek. "I will take your approval first, okay? I won't marry her until you agree."

His sister had done exactly that. Avantika, younger to Vidyut by three years, had married the love of her life, Shatrughan Maheshwari, only after her parents had agreed. It hadn't been the case in the beginning, when Arun and Vandana had been dead set against the match, believing Shatrughan to be a good-for-nothing with no career to speak of.

Vandana sighed, obviously thinking about the same thing. "Why me? First it was Avantika and her beau. Now it is you."

"Why? Are you regretting Avi's marriage to Shatru?" asked Vidyut with a grin, knowing fully well that it was exactly the opposite.

"Don't be silly, Vidu. You very well know that we couldn't have got a better husband for Avantika," said Arun.

"Doesn't that simply mean you should trust your children's judgement better, *Appa*?" he asked, giving his father a wink.

Arun pushed back his chair to get up. "I don't really know what to say, Vidu. You people never listen to me anymore. I suppose it's because I am a retired man and you don't value me any longer." Grumbling, he walked across to sit down on the hall sofa, switching on the TV; not noticing mother and son smiling at each other.

Vidyut came back to the present as he parked his Audi in the twin-car garage. Letting himself into the house, he was glad to see that both his parents were awake. "Hi *Amma, Appa.* How was your day?" he asked.

Arun switched off the TV when he saw his son enter the house, giving him a frown. "You are working really long hours, Vidu," he said, concern in his voice.

On his way to the staircase, Vidyut changed direction to go and kneel in front of his father. "Yes, *Appa.* But I am not complaining. The café is doing really well."

"You are smelling of coffee," said his mother, wrinkling her nose.

Vidyut grinned, getting up. "Talking of which, I left the packet in the car. I got something for you guys." He quickly walked out of the front door, leaving it open. He returned a couple of minutes later carrying two small cardboard boxes in a paper bag. "You have had dinner?"

"Yes," said Arun, eyeing the bag curiously.

"Good. Now you can have this dessert." He opened the bag to hand one box each to his parents, along with biodegradable spoons.

"What about you? Don't you want dinner?" asked Vandana as she opened the box to look inside, giving a squeal of delight when she saw the large slice of cake within. "What is this, Vidu?" she asked.

Arun was already spooning a piece into his mouth, munching on it with relish, nodding his head in approval. "I must say that your chef is good."

Laughing, Vidyut told his mother, "It's orange meringue, using fresh oranges." Turning to his father, he said, "I am the chef, *Appa*."

"Are you serious?" asked Arun, the spoon midway between the cake box and his mouth, utterly surprised.

Vidyut laughed some more. "That's right, *Appa*. My speciality is coffee blends and baking."

"This is so delicious, Vidu," said his mother, getting up to hug her son. "I am so proud of you."

"This is simply too good, Vidu. But I am getting a mite worried about your long working hours," said his father.

Vidyut sat next to his father, taking his hand in his. "I was going to talk to you about it. Do you want to listen?"

"What?" Arun looked at his son, even as he licked his spoon clean. "What do you charge for a piece of this pastry?" he asked.

"Two hundred and twenty rupees, including tax,"

"People pay that kind of money?" Arun gave his son a shocked look.

"People are ready to pay more, actually. I am keeping the costs reasonable. Getting back to the point, do you want to do the accounts for my café? You don't have to come in every day; just two-three days in a week; whenever it suits you."

"Why? How much money are you making that you can't manage it yourself?" Arun asked his son, not having much faith in anything other than a job which paid a monthly income. After all, how many people will throw away hard-earned money on such an expensive piece of cake? The old-fashioned Arun didn't have much faith in this kind of a business.

"The turnover is about three to four lakhs a day, *Appa*," said Vidyut in a quiet voice, "and there are cash as well as card transactions. I am trying my best to manage, but there's only so much time I have. It's also the reason for my long hours. If you aren't interested, I will have to employ someone else soon."

Arun stared at his son, opening and closing his mouth several times, too astounded to say anything. He finally found his voice to ask, "Are you serious? And what kind of profit will that be?"

"Forty percent approximately, after paying the salaries."

Arun shook his head in a daze. "I don't really know what to say!"

Vidyut grinned at his father. "You can tell me that you are proud of being my father," he said mischievously, throwing his arm around Arun's shoulders. "So, are you interested in handling the accounts for Kamath's Koffee?"

"Try and stop me." Arun hugged his son right back, his eyes shimmering with unshed tears. "And yes, my son, I am absolutely proud of you." He kissed Vidyut on his forehead.

idyut stepped out into the restaurant to peep at the crowd with a broad smile on his face. It gave him immense joy to keep checking if the customers kept coming. Of course, the rate at which the food disappeared from the kitchen already told him that. But still, watching people walking in and placing orders truly warmed his heart. He could see that the student-cum-waiters who were taking orders and serving customers were also upbeat.

Turning his head to the right, he was surprised to see Haasini at the corner table, same as yesterday. She was working on her laptop, sipping on a cold coffee. Without thinking twice, he walked over to her table and said, "Hey!"

Lifting her gaze from the laptop, she saw Vidyut and gave him a wide smile, her whole face lighting up. "Hey! I don't have to ask you how your café is doing today," she said, laughter bubbling in her voice.

Finding her mirth infectious, he laughed as well. "That's right. You can see it for yourself. How are you today?"

She shrugged, inadvertently drawing his attention to her bobbing breasts. "I'm good. I was hoping to catch you sometime today for an interview."

He lifted his brows, surprised to hear that. "I thought you were done with your article yesterday." But he was glad she was back here at his coffee shop today, enjoying her presence.

"That was for the newspaper. I want to do an interview for my blog and my YouTube channel."

"That's awesome. Anytime you tell me."

"In half an hour? I am just finishing this piece which I need to send off like yesterday," she grimaced.

"Sure. Just ping me." He lifted his hand in a wave and walked away, unaware of her eyes on his back.

Haasini gave a small sigh as she sat back in her chair, stretching her legs under the table. What was it about the man that made her heart thump madly? He must be much older than she was, at least in his early thirties. She had checked his LinkedIn account and read the long list of educational qualifications; the part-time and full-time jobs he had held in the USA and later in India; until Kamath's Koffee. While there was no year of birth mentioned, it must have taken him that many years to achieve what he had.

Tch!

She didn't have a hope in hell that he might show interest in her. Turning to her laptop, she read the last para she had typed before continuing to tap away at the keys.

Vidyut walked around in a circle before going up the stairs, smiling to himself at the chattering crowd. Everyone had some kind of food item or drink in front of them. Good! Business was booming. Better yet, he was excited that he baked cakes and savouries day after day. He had even added small pizzas—four inches in diameter—with different toppings, to the menu. As he made his own pizza bread, the size worked out well as they were uncommon in the market. But then, the size was ideal for a small meal along with a beverage. As of now, he had four toppings on offer, two vegetarian options and two non-vegetarian ones. Maybe more could be added in the future.

He stopped when his phone buzzed in the back pocket of his jeans. Pulling it out, he saw it was Nirmal. "Hi! Tell me."

"Sir, the pastries are almost gone. Just one piece each left of the strawberry cake and lemon meringue. Could you whip up more anytime soon?"

"In ten minutes. On my way." He swiftly walked down the steps, smiling at a few girls and boys on their way up to the first floor. Vidyut had already baked the bases for the four types of pastries on offer for the next day. He just needed to add the flavoured toppings which shouldn't take him long. As he entered the kitchen, his phone buzzed again.

"Haasini! I have to whip up some pastries urgently. Will you be able to wait or do you need to be somewhere else?"

"I can wait if you'll let me see you work your magic and promise to give me a taste," she gurgled, unable to stop the flirtatious note in her voice.

"Come along to the kitchen, then. Nirmal will let you in." Disconnecting his phone, he quickly set to work at his counter in one corner.

"I think I'm going to get high on sugar if I keep visiting your café like this." Haasini stood next to Vidyut as she watched his large hands while he added cream to the cakes. With long fingers, his movements were minimal and efficient. She had a sudden vision of the same hands on her body, touching her everywhere. A shiver ran down her spine before Haasini got a grip on her runaway thoughts and focused on the questions she had for him. "How many types of cakes do you make?" she asked.

"We have a dozen cakes on the menu, though only four flavours are on offer on a given day." He talked even as he continued to work on the cakes, without turning to give her a glance, completely focused on what he was doing.

"Do all of them get sold at the end of the day?"

He turned then to give her a charming grin, the dimples coming into play much to her fascination. "It's barely one o' clock and the stock I made for today is over."

Her eyes went wide on hearing that. "Should I even ask you how many cakes you made for today?"

"Go ahead and ask," he said, turning back to his counter.

"Tell me." She moved closer to him in the pretext of hearing him better. Or that's what she told herself.

"Each cake makes eight servings. I made forty cakes for today, in four different flavours." He turned suddenly to call out, "Nirmal, the cake menu needs to be changed to the flavours I was planning for tomorrow."

"Already done, sir." Nirmal raised a hand to his boss as he walked out with a heavily laden tray.

"You mean you sold three hundred and twenty slices just this morning?" Haasini's eyes were wide with wonder. "I never got to taste any," she grumbled.

"Not to worry. There's a slice of strawberry cake and one of lemon meringue. What's your preference?" he asked her indulgently, conscious of her closeness, her head almost touching his shoulder. He curbed a sudden urge to kiss her on her cheek, trying to keep his attention on the cream cheese frosting he was applying to a red velvet cake.

"Strawberry! I love them." She smacked her lips. "Please save it for me. But I insist on paying."

He gave her a corner eyed glance before shrugging. "I don't see why you should. Feel free to be as honest as you want in your writeup," he said, tongue-in-cheek, too confident that no one could find fault with the food at Kamath's Koffee.

She poked her tongue at him. "That I plan to be. I'll hold the questions until you finish what you're doing, I think; don't want to break your concentration."

"Hmm," he grunted, "thanks."

She stood next to him, not uttering a word as she watched him decorating cake after cake before slicing them neatly to pass them to Seema who was manning the counter that day.

He was done within a little more than an hour. Haasini didn't mind waiting as she sipped on a glass of freshly squeezed orange juice Nirmal thrust into her hand while watching Vidyut work on not just the cakes but also removing batches of freshly baked pizzas. She was fascinated by the small size, inhaling the captivating aroma of melted cheese and veggies, exclaiming before she could stop herself, "From where did you get those small pizzas? I've never seen any in that size before."

Vidyut turned to give her a smile before sliding the pizzas on to a cooling rack. "I have customised them for Kamath's. The portion is not too big mainly to ensure that people don't waste it. It also gives the customers a chance to taste a variety, while keeping the cost reasonable."

She nodded, impressed despite herself. The man was a genius, surely. "It's similar to how you serve a single piece of *idli* or *vada* as against serving a plate of two."

"Exactly. The cost is halved."

"Does it benefit you?" She looked at him sharply.

"You mean financially?" he asked, walking along with her to the restaurant area now that he was done in the kitchen, continuing to talk when she nodded in affirmation, "It's bound to benefit in the long run. And that's what my restaurant is all about. I want people to come back, again and again."

"Are you ready for the interview?" she asked, sitting down in front of her laptop.

He shrugged. "Why not?"

"I hope you don't mind if I record a video on my phone?"

"Should I go check my appearance in the mirror? I don't want any cream or flour sticking to my face," he joked.

Looking him up and down and liking what she saw, Haasini replied, "You'll do."

"Thank you, kind lady." Vidyut laughed as he sat down in the opposite chair.

She was thorough, asking him loads of questions about not just his restaurant, but also how he landed up being a café owner. Vidyut was frank with his answers, not really making an effort to impress, but simply sharing his journey with her.

After two hours, she said, "Thanks for that. We are done."

"Phew! I did begin to wonder…" His brown eyes crinkled with laughter.

"About what?" she asked, lifting an eyebrow at him.

"You can't deny that it was a pretty long interview."

She shrugged. "Of course, it was. Don't you want people to know all about your restaurant as well as yourself?"

"Hmm… I suppose. To be truthful, I hadn't given it much thought. Thanks a ton, Haasini. It was fun." He got up to shake her hand. "Do tell me if you need any more info."

Holding her right hand which had been engulfed in his palm for a few seconds, even as she wondered if it would ever feel the same again after the electric shock it had received, Haasini gave him a nod, having lost her voice completely.

He walked away, dragging his steps, feeling a strange reluctance to part company with the young woman who had been such an inherent part of his restaurant these last three days. She had asked him so much and he had told her a lot about his dreams and aspirations. So much so, that he suddenly felt a sense of loss. After all, they didn't move in the same circles or he would have met her before, wouldn't he?

Would I ever meet her again?

Vidyut wasn't to know that Haasini had chosen to make Kamath's Koffee her daily place of work. She loved the ambience a lot and the food and beverages even more. It also fitted in her budget, while giving her some space away from her family. Better than all that was the fact that it was just a ten-minute walk from her house. It couldn't be more perfect!

9

It was five days later in the morning and Haasini was in a tearing hurry. She quickly swallowed the piping hot filter coffee and refused the breakfast her mother offered. "I need to go, Mom." She had to final proof an article before sending it off to a newspaper and she would need at least an hour to chop it down to the exact word count required.

But having to rush didn't stop her from making sure she was dressed elegantly, in a flaring cotton skirt printed in multiple shades of blue and white batik, matching it with a white button-down collarless top with elbow-length sleeves. Stepping into white leather open toe espadrilles, she snapped the buckles closed before turning to pick up her laptop bag. Instead of her backpack, she had packed her laptop in a stylish tote bag of blue and white to match her clothes the earlier night itself.

Huh! The bag was way too light. She quickly pulled open the zip to dig inside. While the notebook, pens and her wallet were in the bag, she couldn't find her laptop. How was that even possible? Even her laptop charger was right there. She clearly remembered removing her laptop from her backpack and packing it into the tote bag before going to sleep.

Leaving the bag alone, she went to her cupboard to pull out her backpack, just in case she had made a mistake. But the laptop wasn't there either. With a deep frown, Haasini searched every shelf in her cupboard before each nook and cranny in her room. Shit! Her laptop wasn't in her bedroom.

Rushing into the living room, she looked around, on the shelves below the TV and under the centre table. Her laptop couldn't have disappeared into thin air!

Hearing her push and pull the furniture around, Jyothi stepped out of the kitchen. "Haasini! How come you are still here? Didn't you tell me you were in a hurry and wanted to leave without breakfast?" She asked her daughter in a scolding voice. Jyothi didn't like it if any of the family members left home without having the first meal of the day.

"I'm leaving Mom. Once I find my dratted laptop!" Haasini snarled. She never liked to be late for a submission. A typical Cancerian, she was extremely particular about her professional reputation.

"Where did you leave it last night?" asked Jyothi, a deep frown on her face.

"In the tote bag I planned to take with me today," responded Haasini in an impatient voice which grew louder in direct proportion to her rising temper. She wished her mother would stop distracting her with her questions.

"What's going on?" Haresh stepped out from his room, all ready to go to work. "Why are you both shouting?"

"Haasini can't find her laptop," provided Jyothi in an irritated voice. "If you can go late, why not eat your breakfast? Where's the need to starve?" she muttered, turning towards the kitchen.

Haasini decided to ignore her mother as she spoke to her father. "My laptop has strangely disappeared, Dad. I remember packing it in my tote bag last night."

Haresh's face turned dark with temper, his mind flashing back to the scene in the middle of last night. He had happened to step out of his room probably around 2 AM and had noticed Janani going into Haasini's room. He hadn't thought much of it as there was nothing strange about one sister visiting the other, even if it was so late in the night. Could it be possible that it was Janani who had done something to Haasini's laptop?

He quickly turned right, crossed the kitchen doorway, and went inside Janani's room. He opened her wardrobe and wasn't really surprised to see a laptop sitting on the top shelf. He knew for a fact that Janani didn't own one. Taking it down, he carried it to the living room, calling to Haasini, "See if this is yours?"

"Dad! You are a life saviour." Haasini placed a hand on his shoulder to give him a loud kiss on his cheek. "This is mine. Where did you find it?"

Even her affectionate kiss didn't remove the black frown from Haresh's face. He realised that his elder daughter had played the mischief; and deliberately too. What was the need for it? It wasn't as if it was a simple prank. Haasini needed her laptop to do her work. And Janani had taken off to her school after hiding it in her cupboard. What a horrid thing to do!

Without divulging the fact regarding Janani's mischief mongering, Haresh asked Haasini, "Does it matter? Weren't you in a hurry?"

"Oh yes, Dad! Thanks a ton." She rushed back into her room to shove the laptop into her bag and rushed out again, blowing kisses to both her parents as she almost ran out of the house.

"Did she find the laptop?" asked Jyothi who had just stepped out in time to wave to Haasini.

"I did," said Haresh in an ominous voice. He poured a glass of chilled water from the fridge and drank it down in gulps, hoping to calm his shattered nerves. What the hell was happening? Why had Janani done what she had done?

"*You* found the laptop?" asked Jyothi in a surprised voice as she stared at her husband. "Where was it?"

"In Janani's wardrobe, on the top shelf."

Jyothi lost the colour in her face. "Are you serious?"

Haresh shrugged. "Good question. If I hadn't seen it for myself, I might have asked the same question too. Last night, you forgot to keep a bottle of water at my bedside. I..."

What was the connection? Jyothi glared at her husband. "I am sorry about that. But I am only human..."

He shook his head vigorously. "Listen! I wasn't complaining. Because of that, I went out of our room to get a bottle from the fridge. That's when I saw Janani going into Haasini's room. Just now, when Haasini told me she couldn't find her laptop, I automatically went to Janani's room to check. And there it was, lying on the top shelf of her cupboard."

Jyothi placed both her hands on her mouth, one over the other, her wide eyes shocked. "But... but Haasini needs the laptop to do her work every day. Doesn't Janani know that?"

"If you as a housewife can realise that, your educated elder daughter must jolly well understand that." Haresh was beyond furious by now. It was obvious to him that his elder born was trying to mess up his younger one's life. Talk about an idle mind being a devil's workshop. The few hours she worked at the school was obviously not enough of an occupation for Janani, it seemed. It was probably not mentally stimulating either. Something had to be done about it; and soon.

Even as she swiftly walked towards Kamath's Koffee, Haasini's mind revolved around the article she needed to submit that day. While it was going to be used in their Sunday edition, the newspaper expected her to submit it by Friday first half, that is, in another couple of hours.

Checking the slim watch on her wrist, she took a deep breath even as she stepped up her pace. It was half past ten already. Damn it! She couldn't help wondering how her laptop had managed to leave her room. The wonder was that her father had found it immediately. Had he borrowed it for something?

She mentally shrugged. That must be it! She tended to leave her laptop in 'sleep' mode most of the time and it wouldn't have been difficult for him to use it. *Did he need a laptop? Maybe I should buy him one!* Haasini smiled to herself, feeling proud of the fact that she had managed to earn really good money and saved most of it during the time she spent away from home. Even during the few months when she had lived with Yeshwant, she had not stopped working and had put her foot down when he expected her to pay for the housekeeping expenses. No way! She had told him clearly that she either did the housework or paid her way. She wasn't a fool to do both. Not left with a choice, it was Yeshwant who had footed all the bills.

Haasini could easily afford to buy her father a laptop. That thought pleased her more than anything and she soon forgot her irritation when she stepped into Kamath's Koffee. The thought of meeting its owner cheered her up no end. Vidyut made her heart soar and it felt as if she was floating on air whenever he smiled at her. That they had spoken nothing beyond their work didn't matter to Haasini. After all, it had been only a few weeks after her return to Bengaluru. Time enough to get to know him better. The café was closed on Mondays, which obviously must be his day off. Dying to know about Vidyut's personal life, she planned to tackle him on the coming Monday.

Stepping into the café, Haasini turned to the left only to find her table—that's how she had begun to look at the corner table next to the window—occupied. Grimacing, she looked around, searching for another cosy corner.

"Hello, ma'am, good morning. Are you looking for a table?" asked Nirmal, helpfully, giving her a broad smile.

"Hi Nirmal, good morning. Yes. Mine's gone," she stated the obvious, her lips drooping.

"There's a window table on the first floor, right above this one. Shall I see if it's free?"

"Don't bother, Nirmal. I'll find it. Let me order something first." The first floor usually had a few free tables at this time of the day. But the chances of meeting Vidyut were bound to be less. With a soft sigh, Haasini turned to the counter. Stopping suddenly, she turned to Nirmal and said, "Can you do me a favour? Ping me on my phone when the table gets empty, will you?"

"I'll do that, ma'am, for sure," he said, quickly taking out his phone to save her number before giving her a missed call.

Cheering up, she placed her order for a plate of *idli-vada* and filter coffee; craving for the taste of South Indian food that morning. Which was exactly the reason why she had avoided eating the *aloo parathas* her mother had prepared for breakfast. Walking up the stairs, she found a table for four right in the middle, which was the only table which was free. Shrugging, she settled down, swiftly getting lost in her work.

Janani was in an excessively jolly mood that day, so much so that some of the other primary teachers in the school gave her surprised glances as if they wondered what was going on.

But then, Janani was feeling thrilled that she had found a way to thwart her younger sister. She had been awake late into the night, wondering how to irritate Haasini who appeared so chirpy while both the parents gave her a lot of attention. It looked as if they had forgotten how their younger daughter had eloped with a good-for-nothing man when she had been barely twenty. They seemed to have forgotten the shame they had had to undergo while facing relatives and friends.

But Janani hadn't forgotten, not one bit of it. Her mother had cried day after day until there were no more tears left. Her father had taken his temper out by shouting at his wife, day in and day out, blaming her for Haasini's guts.

Which was so unfair! Haasini was a brat, through and through. Not at all like her elder sister, Janani, who was so sweet and well-behaved. Janani never crossed the line, always listening to her parents and respecting all elders. Why, hadn't she listened to them and agreed to marry Vidyut Kamath? And later broken the engagement, only because they didn't approve of his changed profession?

What she hadn't expected was for her stupid parents to fall for Haasini's professed charm all over again. Come on, they had not even scolded her for leaving them high and dry two years ago. How dumb was that!

That was why Janani decided to teach her younger sister the lesson of her life. Hiding her laptop, without which Haasini wouldn't be able to carry on with her career, was the first step.

Janani covered her mouth with a hand as a bright smile widened her lips when she got out of the rickshaw outside her home. She knew for a fact that Haasini must be furious as she paced their living room, totally lost without her laptop. Serve her right!

She let herself into the bungalow and was surprised to be greeted by the emptiness and silence. Where was Haasini? And her mother for that matter? It was barely two in the afternoon.

"Mom!" Not finding Jyothi in the kitchen, Janani went to her parents' bedroom in search of her mother. "Mom!"

Jyothi looked up from the book she was reading to glare at her elder daughter. "Why are you shouting? It's loud enough to wake the dead," she snarled.

Janani couldn't believe her ears as it was extremely rare for Jyothi to speak so harshly. What was wrong with her mother? "Are you upset about something, Mom?" she asked, going to sit on the bed beside her mother and placing a hand on her shoulder. "And is there no one else at home?" she continued, wondering about Haasini.

Haresh had left strict instructions to his wife that he was going to return from work and have a chat with Janani and Jyothi wasn't to open her mouth until then about the laptop. But that didn't stop Jyothi from burning with anger. She was totally convinced that Janani was up to some kind of mischief. Only, it wasn't the playful kind. There would have been serious repercussions if Haresh had not found Haasini's laptop; her younger daughter's career could have been at stake.

"Who do you expect to be home at this time of the afternoon?" asked Jyothi sharply.

"Um… er… no one, I suppose. I just asked," said Janani, dying of curiosity to know about Haasini's whereabouts.

Jyothi huffed, returning to her book. "The food is on the dining table. Help yourself."

Janani was astounded. Her mother never, but never, behaved like this. She always went and sat with Janani when she had her lunch. Why was she acting like this today? Had Haasini said something? But then, Haasini wouldn't know that it was Janani who had hidden her laptop. So, what was Jyothi pissed off about?

It was a few minutes to seven when Haresh returned home from work. His face was thunderous when he saw Janani sitting in the living room, watching some serial on TV.

"Hello, Dad!" she called out cheerfully, removing a bottle of water from the fridge and handing it to him.

Haresh didn't return her greeting as he drank the water. Handing the half-empty bottle back to her, he swiftly went to his room to change, only too aware of his daughter's startled glance following him. Good! Let her stew!

Jyothi carried a tray with three cups of coffee and a plateful of homemade *kodubale*, a crunchy and spicy fried snack special to the region, and placed it on the centre table.

"What's Dad upset about?" asked Janani, an avid expression on her face. "Did Haasini do something to irritate you both?" she continued eagerly, dying to have her sister's name blackened in her parents' eyes once again.

"It's you who has irritated us," said Haresh as he stepped out of his room. Sitting on the sofa, he took the remote and switched off the TV. Munching on a piece of *kodubale*, he met Janani's gaze directly. "What was Haasini's laptop doing in your cupboard?"

Aah! So that's why Haasini was not at home; all because they had found the hidden laptop. Tch! *It had been a mistake not locking my cupboard and taking the key with me.* Janani didn't answer her father as she concentrated on picking a cup of coffee and sipping from it.

"I asked you a question." Haresh's voice became a harsh growl even as his temper escalated.

"Hmm... I am trying to answer you, Dad. Let me finish my coffee before it goes cold." She needed time to think; to come up with an excuse that would ensure her parents didn't come after her. *Che!* It looked like her plan had backfired. "Who found the laptop?" she asked, looking at her silent mother before turning to her father.

"Does it matter? What is of significance is that the laptop which Haasini had left in her bag, in her bedroom, had found its way into your cupboard..." He lifted an eyebrow, inviting an explanation from her.

"Is that what Haasini told you?" Janani's brain worked slowly. She wasn't quick on her feet when it came to building stories. She was a planner, but not one to consider all the angles before doing something.

Haresh had a difficult time not slapping his elder born as he drank his coffee in silence, his dark eyes pinning her as he continued to glare at her; as if he could force the truth out of Janani if he did that. "Not really."

What kind of an answer was that? Janani looked at her father warily. Who could have found the laptop? And how did they manage to trace it to her wardrobe? She was confused.

Haresh knew that Janani could be as stubborn as a mule and had a mean streak as well. For all her fire and rebellion, Haasini had a good heart. He was keen that Janani confess to her part in the laptop scenario, but it was obvious that she was only stalling for time. "Forget about Haasini. What do you have to say about it, Janani? Why did you take her laptop? Don't you know that Haasini needs it to do her work?" He was having an extremely tough time speaking calmly as all he wanted to do was shout at her.

Janani sat back on the sofa, doing her best to give the appearance of being cool while in truth she was seething inside. It was obvious that her father was taking Haasini's side, without even listening to her—Janani's—version. How unfair was that?! She conveniently forgot that she hadn't answered him when he asked her for an explanation. Giving him an angry glance, she accused, "You always take her side!"

Jyothi saw red! Jumping up from the sofa, she snarled, "You idiot! This is not a fight between you and Haasini. Haasini isn't even aware that the laptop was in your wardrobe. It was your father who found it. We both know it was you who had taken the laptop. All your father is asking is why."

"I have no privacy in this house. I wonder who dared to search my wardrobe! From now on I am going to lock my room whenever I am not at home."

"You wouldn't dare! This house belongs to me!" Haresh's voice rose up by many notches.

Her chin trembling even as her eyes filled, Janani got up from her seat, looking at her parents. "You hate me, both of you. You only love Haasini who has the morals of an alley cat. You have forgotten how she ran away with that useless man from next door and lived with him. She is a whore! That's what she is!" The next second, she held her burning cheek, having been dealt a hard slap by her mother.

"Should I call you a thief for taking Haasini's laptop without her knowledge or permission?" Haresh snarled at his daughter, unmoved by her tears. She hadn't given him a straightforward answer for that one, yet.

"Am I not her sister? Can't I borrow her laptop?" Janani was screaming now.

"Without her knowledge? Taking it from her in the middle of the night? Who does that?" Haresh was relentless.

"Middle of the night?" Janani forgot to cry as she stared at her father. How did he know that? Did they have a CCTV camera fitted in the house, maybe?

"You might as well admit to it, Janani. I saw you going into Haasini's room last night," said Haresh in a disgusted voice. "Now get away from my sight. I can't believe a daughter of mine can behave in such a fashion."

"Is it okay if your other daughter elopes with a stranger and returns after two years, without even marrying him?" Janani glared at her father before going to her room and shutting the door with a loud bang.

She swore to herself that she would get Haasini for this, the bitch!

Jyothi looked helplessly at Haresh after Janani flounced off to her room to sulk. "I never thought… I never expected. Where did we go wrong?" she asked in a voice trembling with emotion. "First, Haasini ran away. And now, Janani is behaving so weirdly."

Haresh sighed. "I was terribly upset and angry when Haasini ran away then. But, somehow, I am unable to hold on to my anger towards her. She was an innocent and had been led astray by that stupid moron Yeshwant. But look at her now. Only two years away from home, but she has become so mature and responsible."

Jyothi nodded. "That's so true. It feels as if she had been studying in another city and is back home now; more confident and calmer than before."

"But look at Janani. She's holding such dislike and envy in her heart. Otherwise, why would she hide Haasini's laptop?" Haresh shook his head, flummoxed by Janani's behaviour. They had always treated the girls equally.

"I notice that Janani has not spoken one word to Haasini since she returned home," said Jyothi, her lips drooping pathetically.

Haresh gave a slow nod. "I noticed it too. That's why I feel Janani doesn't like Haasini, not at all. But why this hatred? It isn't as if Janani's prospects were spoilt because Haasini eloped with some guy. Her marriage was fixed to one of the best bachelors in Bengaluru." He sighed deeply. "I only wish she hadn't been so hasty in breaking off the engagement. I can't help wondering if we would even find someone of the same calibre as Vidyut Kamath."

"And you know something?" Jyothi was quick to point out, "There was such a big article in Friday's issue of some newspaper, all about his coffee shop, I believe. There were even three pictures, it seems. Sushila called up to tell me. We have made a mistake there, Haresh."

His sigh was louder than before. Jyothi's nosy friend would have been only too keen on pointing out the error of their ways. But, to be honest, he said, "I can't agree more. Janani shouldn't have returned his ring like that. She's not left a leg for me to stand on. I can't even go and patch things up with them after her behaviour." Neither

Haresh nor Jyothi were aware that it was their younger daughter who had written the article.

"So, it's all my fault now, isn't it?" Janani shouted from where she was standing halfway down the living room. She had creeped out of her room to eavesdrop on her parents' conversation and didn't care for what they were discussing. "Dad, you told me to go meet Vidyut. And tell him to stop his restaurant nonsense and go back to work. I passed your message. But the bull-headed Taurus that he is, he refused to listen to me."

"Are you saying you gave him an ultimatum?" asked Haresh in a shocked voice. What an idiot!

"Of course I did! Isn't that what you told me to do?" asked Janani defiantly.

"I give up!" Haresh threw his arms in the air. "Do what you want. You can find your own husband. I refuse to get involved."

"You are being mean to me, Dad," said Janani in an accusing voice, glaring at him.

Haresh looked helplessly at his wife, not knowing what to say in response to his daughter. He couldn't make out whether she was just ignorant or a complete fool.

Catching his morose expression, Jyothi said, "Janani, don't talk disrespectfully to your father. He was only saying how you could have handled the situation with more tact."

"Oh yeah! Blame me for everything when things go wrong." She walked back into her room and once again banged the door loudly in protest.

Jyothi placed a pacifying hand on her bristling husband's arm. "Calm down, will you? Let's leave her alone for some time. I am sure she will come around once she stops being angry."

But Janani was too blinded by jealousy and wasn't going to calm down in a hurry; her hatred towards her younger sister festering deeper than ever.

10

Ultimately, it took Haasini just about an hour to complete proofreading her article before sending it to the newspaper. Taking a deep breath, she sat back in her chair, savouring a second cup of coffee as she stared out of the window unseeingly even as she wondered where Vidyut was.

She had got so used to meeting him every day by now as he stopped at her table for a quick chat, a smile bringing his dimples into play. Haasini had stopped being bothered by her palpitating heart as that had become an everyday affair beginning from the moment she stepped into the premises of Kamath's Koffee.

But today, it was almost an hour and a half after she had settled on the first floor and still there was no sight nor sound of the owner. Was he busy in the kitchen? She wouldn't be surprised as orders for the baked goods were placed non-stop, it seemed. He sure had a tight schedule; and appeared to really enjoy what he was doing.

Which left next to no time for them to get to know one another. And that's exactly why she planned to catch him on his weekly holiday. It was just that Monday seemed so far off.

She sighed, her lips drooping at the corners.

"Hey! Is everything okay?" asked Vidyut, hearing her sigh as he slid into the seat across from her.

Haasini's face lit up like a Christmas tree. "Hey yourself! You're having a busy morning."

So true! When he stepped out of his kitchen for a breather, Vidyut refused to admit to a sense of disappointment when he couldn't find Haasini in her regular corner downstairs. And it was by chance he had come up to this floor to simply gaze at his customers having a good time. The feeling of excitement which made his heart thud heavily was inordinate in its unexpectedness when he caught sight of Haasini sitting alone at a table for four.

Did she appear more beautiful than before or was it his imagination going into overdrive?!

Suddenly remembering her words, he nodded. "Yep. So, you tell me! What was that long sigh all about?"

She shrugged. "Just! Can't wait for the week to end."

"Too much work to do?" he asked, his voice concerned as he eyed her in the white top. It made her skin glow. Not waiting for her answer, he asked, "Going somewhere? You are all decked up."

She lifted a shapely brow at him, her elbow on the table with her chin in her hand. *Whatever did he mean by that? Wasn't she here at his coffee shop? Wasn't that going somewhere?* "Not really."

"You look lovely." The words escaped his lips before he could stop himself. Though she was here at the café every day, they had really chatted on only two occasions. *Will she resent his familiarity?*

Haasini smiled widely. "Thanks." Phew! He had noticed.

That hadn't been too bad! "So, what are you reviewing today?"

"A movie. Ajay Devgan's *Tanhaji*." She wrinkled her nose in distaste.

"Not good?" he asked, sipping from his mug.

"Two and a half stars."

"Oh! That bad?"

She laughed. "You don't need to be so upset about it. It has its pluses and minuses."

"Balanced review, eh?" he grinned.

"You know something? You have the cutest dimples I've ever seen." Haasini couldn't stop herself from telling it to his face and was totally fascinated when she noticed the dark colour rushing up his rugged cheeks. "I didn't know a guy could blush," she said, her voice a fascinated whisper.

His smile disappearing, Vidyut shook his head at her, rendered completely speechless for probably the first time in his life.

She felt disappointed when the dimples vanished along with his smile. Setting off at a tangent, she said, "I need to review a discotheque the coming week. Do you dance?"

Vidyut gave her a curious glance, wondering where the conversation was going. "Hmm."

"Will you go with me?"

Wouldn't he love to spend some time with her? Vidyut didn't really have to think before he answered, "Late night works for you? Say around 10.30 or so. I can't leave until the café shuts for the night."

"Can't you delegate?" she asked, curious.

He shrugged. "Maybe after a few months. It's still too new."

"Hmm, I guess. Next Wednesday works for you?"

"Okay. And thanks for inviting me along," he said, giving her a winning smile.

"It's my pleasure." He got up with obvious reluctance when his phone pinged. "I've to go. I'll see you around."

"Ciao." While she called out cheerfully to his retreating figure, Haasini was unhappy. With no urgent work to drive her, she felt at a loose end and wouldn't have minded his company for some more time. Feeling moody, she glared at her phone when it pinged. Tch! It was some mail; nothing important.

She didn't want to go home. She had no friends in Bengaluru. All the ones she had known had shifted to other cities; some even to different countries. The only sibling she had was Janani. The fact was that they never got along. Not before; not now. Haasini could not really understand why Janani disliked her so. No, she wasn't going to use the dreaded "hate" word. After all, it required a lot of energy.

Her mind went around to the many times Janani had quarrelled with her. There were even a few times when her elder sister had physically attacked her—slapping her hard and pulling her hair harder. It was during the times both the parents hadn't been around. Haasini suddenly realised Janani had always ensured she wasn't caught in the act.

Was it one of the reasons why Haasini had felt the urge to flee her home? She stared at her laptop screen unseeingly. Why give Janani so much power over her?

Haasini shook her head to herself. She had been seeking fun and adventure and had run away with Yeshwant for a lark, not really considering the consequences. And that was the simple fact!

She sighed, her spirits sinking low. *Should I catch a movie? No*, Haasini answered her own question, *not so soon after Tanhaji*. The fact was that she was bored and lonely, sitting here in the middle of the crowded coffee shop.

She quickly scanned the moon chart and saw that it was waning. No wonder! The waning moon always made her mood nosedive. Which was like half of every month.

Damn and a double damn!

Just knowing about it made her mood worse than before. Haasini felt so frustrated that she wanted to throw something badly. She clutched her hands into tight fists, gritting her teeth so hard that her jaw ached with the tension. How the hell do I deal with this?

The ringing of her phone brought her morbid thoughts to a halt. It was Nirmal. "Hi."

"Ma'am! We are adding a new item to the menu. Vidyut sir asked me to find out if you are interested in visiting the kitchen. And by the way, your corner table is emptying as we talk, if you want to shift your things downstairs."

"Nirmal! Thanks a ton!" He had just saved her from a situation worse than death. "I owe you one." She blew him a kiss before disconnecting, unaware of the lifelong loyalty she had garnered from Vidyut's second-in-command. Stuffing her laptop into her bag, she thrust her feet into her espadrilles and took the stairs two at a time to reach the ground floor in a jiffy. Dropping her tote bag on the corner table, she paused to catch her breath before walking to the kitchen at a slower pace.

Nirmal greeted her with an extra warm smile when he opened the door to the kitchen.

"What are you guys inaugurating today?"

"Vidyut sir will tell you," responded Nirmal mysteriously. He had his reasons as the announcement hadn't yet been made to the public.

"Hi! Come Haasini. I thought you wouldn't want to miss this."

"Miss what?" she asked, dying of curiosity, her blue mood forgotten as if it hadn't existed.

"*Bele obattu*! We are inaugurating the local version of *puran poli* today." He spoke in the tone of a magician pulling a rabbit out of a hat as he grinned at her.

"Whaaaaatttttt! Really!" Haasini's eyes shone with delight as she first stared at him and then at the tray where about twenty pieces of the sweetmeat lay between layers of white waxed paper cut into squares. "Whoa!" she said in an awed whisper.

"Impressive, aren't they? Ramu *anna* is a prized discovery," he said proudly before introducing the two. "Ramu *anna*, this is Haasini Rai, a writer. And Haasini, Ramu *anna* was working at a 5-star in Mysuru before I persuaded him to join Kamath's Koffee."

"Ramu *anna*!" gasped Haasini, "It's wonderful meeting you again. How do you do?"

Ramu laughed as he deftly turned the *poli* on the iron skillet over the stove. "Haasini! Isn't it a small world! I am all good. So, you are in Bengaluru nowadays, is it?" he asked.

"Yes. I have moved back with my parents. How come you quit your 5-star job?" she asked curiously.

He shrugged. "It was getting too routine and impersonal. Vidyut and I go a long way. The day I got to know he was starting his own café, I applied for a job. It has taken him one whole month to take me on board," said Ramu, his tongue tucked firmly in his cheek.

His arms folded across his chest, Vidyut leaned against the counter watching the two of them chat, an indulgent smile on his face. Ramu was not just a specialist in making *Bele obattu*, but a whole lot of other dishes original to Karnataka. Hiring him was one of the best decisions he had made for his café. But then, he had had to wait for a whole month to be sure of the continuous and heavy footfall at Kamath's Koffee before taking the man on. Otherwise, it would have been too much of a risk to lure the experienced chef away from his 5-star kitchen.

"I had interviewed Ramu *anna* for a festival issue of Mysore Times two years ago," said Haasini, turning to include Vidyut in the conversation.

"She made a celebrity chef out of me," said Ramu, smiling at her.

"Come on, Ramu *anna*, you are exaggerating," protested Haasini, colouring.

"Not at all. I was a regular on twenty episodes of a food show featured by NDTV Good Times only after your interview, Haasini. I am forever grateful for that."

"Oh yeah! I caught most of the episodes, Ramu *anna*. I think I will take your autograph now."

He nodded, his focus on the dish he was preparing.

"How do you decide what the demand is?" asked Haasini, turning to Vidyut, "You really need to keep track of changing tastes, don't you?"

"Which is one more reason why I hired college students for the café. They are clear about what they like and dislike; having no qualms about expressing their opinions. Eh, Nirmal?" Vidyut called out to his head waiter who insisted on putting in two shifts on three days of the week.

"That's true, Vidyut sir. Life's too short to spend time in procrastination," said the young but wise Nirmal. "And traditional dishes are more in demand than ever. Shall I make the announcement on the blackboard?" he asked, turning from Vidyut to Ramu and back again. That was one of the favourite parts of his job, to update the menu board at the back of the billing counter.

"Feel free," said Vidyut, giving his nod. Turning to Haasini, he said, "I hold regular meetings with them and take their views seriously. After all, they are the perfect samples of the kind of people who hang out in coffee shops."

"I see what you mean," said Haasini, eyeing the retreating figure of Nirmal before turning to give Vidyut her full attention. "What about me? You can ask for my opinion any day," she said, grinning at him.

"As a consultant, I suppose. But then, you will give me a huge bill," he said half teasingly.

She laughed, shaking her head. "No, no. I don't know enough to be a consultant and all. I just love poking my nose into things which interest me. As you must know by now, food is one of those."

"Hmm. Will keep that in mind for sure."

"Isn't it difficult to keep track of so many items on the menu?" she asked.

"That's why we don't offer all the items every day. The menu keeps changing depending on the day of the week. In a way, it keeps us all on our toes," he grinned.

"Like six different menus for six days of the week?" she asked, grinning right back as she eyed his dimples.

He nodded. "That's right. It also makes the customers curious enough to return as often as they can."

"You might want to have special menus during festival times," she suggested.

"That's a damn good idea, Haasini. I haven't thought that far. But you are right. It will be a good crowd puller; especially interesting those who are staying away from their homes."

She nodded, "Exactly." She knew from personal experience how much she missed home during festivals. Though she had tried her best to recreate the atmosphere at the homestay in Mysuru where she had lived and cooked. Taking a deep breath, she said enthusiastically, "I was at a loose end. Now let me go and think up ideas for festive menus for Kamath's Koffee."

"Are you sure, Haasini?" Vidyut was extremely strict with his budget and wasn't keen on paying a consultant. He wouldn't mind working on the menu when he had the time.

"Yes, I am. Call it a return gift for providing me with a wonderful workspace not far from home," she called out to him over her shoulder as she walked to the kitchen door. "I'll see you, Ramu *anna*."

Vidyut took a couple of long strides, stopping her in her tracks with his hand on her slender shoulder.

"I'll agree if you promise to take a discount on your orders. Does that work for you?"

Her long eyelashes fluttered rapidly even as her heart jumped to her throat at his touch. She gave him a small nod, unable to utter a single word as her vocal cords were jammed all because of her choked throat.

"Thanks, Haasini," he said, unsmiling as he felt the heat in his hand from where he touched her shoulder. It was such a strange sensation, one that he had never felt before. He stared at his hand once she had stepped out of the kitchen, wondering if it would ever feel the same again.

H aasini was disappointed to see the shutters to the café pulled down when she went there on Monday. She knew it was closed to the public, but somehow, she had expected Vidyut and a few others to be there, getting the place cleaned up and ready for the coming week. She stepped back to lift her head to see if the blinds were open on the first floor only to find them down too.

Just as she turned away from the entrance, a side door opened. "Haasini ma'am!"

She turned in a flash, a wide smile on her face when she saw Nirmal. "Hey! I did wonder if someone was there."

"Come inside, ma'am. Vidyut sir is working in his office." He had rightly assumed she was there to meet the café owner.

"Thanks, Nirmal. Another minute and I would have left."

He nodded, saying, "Come in, ma'am. I just made coffee. Would you like to have some? It's on the house, of course," he grinned.

"I'd love to have some hot coffee," she said, walking inside. Winter had set in and she was dying for a cup. "Where's Vidyut's office?"

"Behind the kitchen, ma'am," said Nirmal, pointing to the door on the left side as they entered the space. "You go in, ma'am. I'll bring your coffee there."

I hope he wouldn't mind my walking in without prior warning. Haasini didn't utter the words even as they came to her mind. It was time to find out. Stepping out of the kitchen, she crossed the washrooms—both "his" and "hers"—before noticing a door facing her at the furthest point in the corridor. Taking a deep breath, she went forward to knock on it.

"Come in." Vidyut's voice was commanding as he invited whoever was outside his door, not bothering to lift his gaze from his laptop where he was feeding information into the accounting software he had set up for the business. "Please sit down and I'll be with you in a minute," he said, pointing to a visitor's chair without looking up.

Haasini followed his instructions and settled down in the chair on the left. She couldn't help but admire his concentration, completely unaware of the lock of hair which had fallen on his forehead, his focus completely on his work. But after another five minutes, she wasn't sure if she should admire him or be miffed with him. How could he continue to work without even being aware of an attractive woman sitting right across his table?

And attractive she definitely was. More so today as Haasini was clad in a blood red sleeveless top over figure hugging jeans; her thick hair left loose and reaching down to her waist.

There was a peremptory knock on the door before Nirmal walked in with a tray which held steaming mugs of coffee and a plate of cookies.

Vidyut immediately stopped working to give his employee a wide smile. "Thanks, buddy!" Noticing Haasini only then, his eyes lit up with pleasure. "Hey, this is a surprise. I didn't realise it was you who had walked in. Or I would…"

"Or you would have done what?" Haasini shook her head at him, pouting prettily. "Are you even aware that I've been sitting here for more than five minutes?" It was an effort to hold back her irritation. But then, she couldn't really blame him, could she? For one thing, he hadn't been expecting her; and for another, he was extremely busy. But this was the first time she had been within five feet of a man and he hadn't even been aware of her presence.

Neither of them noticed when Nirmal walked out of the cabin, shutting the door quietly behind him.

Vidyut smiled, getting up from his chair and walking forward to sit at the corner of his desk, facing her. Lifting a mug of freshly brewed coffee, he offered it to her. She looked sexy in that red top while her legs appeared so slim and long in the figure-hugging jeans. Gorgeous! Wrinkling his nose at her, he apologised, "Sorry, Haasini. I was so deep into the accounts I didn't notice who it was. Believe me when I say that if I had seen you, I would have definitely lost my concentration." He gave her a slow grin which brought his dimples into play, fascinating her no end.

The rough baritone stroked her quivering nerves even as her eyes went wide when she saw him without an apron for the first time. The ink-blue cotton sleeveless t-shirt he wore fitted across his wide and muscular chest as if he had been poured into it, his stomach as flat as a washboard. She clenched her left fist, her hold on the coffee mug tightening as she curbed the sudden urge to caress his well-honed biceps. Her mouth dried up, parching her throat as well before she took a quick gulp of the scalding coffee, her eyes continuing to travel over the cream cotton pants which stretched over the length of his muscular legs. His feet were encased in black sneakers with a neon yellow trim. She didn't miss the bare ankles on show between the hem of the pants and the shoes as it was obvious he wore no socks. All this she noticed in the span of a few seconds, feeling a desperate urge to fan herself as her blood sizzled, making her sweat despite the cool weather.

"Here! Help yourself to some cookies," he offered, lifting the plate from the tray and holding it in front of her.

"Thanks!" she said, her voice hoarse as she took a cookie from the plate. "You made them?"

"Hmm… mmm!" He continued to drink his coffee, his eyes watching her minutely. He didn't know why she was here, only too glad that she was.

"I hope I'm not disturbing you," she said, taking a bite of the coconut flavoured cookie which simply melted in her mouth. "Mmm… this is so yummy. I'm glad I came here today."

"So am I," he said quietly.

Haasini's eyes had been shut as she savoured the cookie, but they came wide open the instant she heard his words. *Does he mean it? That he is glad I am here today?* She didn't voice her thoughts as she looked into his chocolate brown gaze which glowed fierily. "I... I...," she looked down at her hands, unable to meet his gaze any longer. "I was in the area and thought I would come over to say 'hi'. I hope you don't mind."

He shook his head. "And I'm glad you came. You don't need an excuse to visit here, Haasini," he said. "Have one more." He took another cookie in his hand and offered it to her.

Instead of taking it in her hand, Haasini leaned forward to take a bite of it, looking into his eyes.

Reading the invitation in her gaze, he popped the rest of the cookie into his own mouth, giving her a wink, smiling when he saw the colour rush up her face. For all her forwardness, she was an innocent. He sighed. She was also so damn young! Maybe a decade younger than he was. Turning away swiftly, he went to sit in his chair, deciding to keep his distance.

"Wanna go out for lunch? My treat!" she suggested, lifting a challenging brow at him.

"What if your parents object?" he asked, the smile having disappeared from his face. She was a kid, dammit! He felt like a paedophile!

"Huh? Why would they? I am too old to need my parents' permission to go out to lunch with a guy," she snorted.

"You don't look a day over seventeen," he said, half teasingly.

"*Meh!* Do you know any other seventeen-year-old writing reviews for newspapers?" She pouted at him, unaware of the effect it was having on his libido which was leaping out of control.

Vidyut took a deep breath to calm down his rising blood pressure, to no avail. She was too damn cute and was growing on him slowly, but steadily. "Okay, eighteen then. You make me feel ancient," he said in a half-groan.

"Why don't you simply ask my age instead of beating around the bush?" she asked him cheekily.

"Why don't you tell me?" He lifted an eyebrow challengingly.

"Twenty-two years and five months."

"That's really old, I suppose," he said, his voice mildly sarcastic.

"And how old you are, O ancient one?" she asked with full blown sarcasm even as she glared at him, her black eyes spitting fire.

He laughed out loud, unable to stop himself, shaking his head at her. "Thirty and a couple of months."

"Does that mean we are allowed to have lunch together?" she asked, continuing to glare at him.

"Now how can I refuse such an offer? Only if you'll let me pay the bill, though."

She poked her tongue at him, the juvenile gesture only confirming how young she was. Getting up from her chair, she turned towards the door. "I'll pick you up at one," she threw over one slender shoulder before walking out.

He was shaking with laughter, thoroughly entertained by her behaviour. Yes, she was too damn young! But what the hell! He liked her a lot and planned to enjoy himself at lunch. It was an effort, but he forced himself to complete the work he had set out to do, startled when his phone rang just as he was shutting his laptop.

Seeing Haasini's face on the screen, he took the call to say, "Hello." It was exactly one pm.

"I'm outside your café, in a cab. Are you ready to leave?"

"In ten. Would you mind terribly if we go in my car?" he asked, grinning at his laptop.

"Okay! I'll let the cab go in that case."

"Why don't you come inside? I need ten minutes before I can leave."

"Fine."

"I'll see you," he said, laughing again as he disconnected the call. Vidyut realised he had missed feminine company all this long. And he had to admit Haasini was all woman despite the way he teased her about being a little more than a kid.

Vidyut handed his car key over to the valet at the entrance to Stories, Brewery & Kitchen on Lake Road, BTM, before taking Haasini's hand in his. He couldn't help thinking about Janani, the woman he had been betrothed to for no less than six months. He had never had the guts to take her hand in his. As for Haasini, he had met her a few times and had chatted a lot with her while she interviewed him. Despite all that, they didn't know each other very well. And there was the age difference of almost eight years. How come he felt no qualms holding her hand? By now, Vidyut was ready to let go of her hand only to find her fingers firmly entwined with his.

And the way his body reacted! Damn! The timing couldn't be worse for his libido to wake up—and with a vengeance too—after more than two years!

The place was just filling up when they stepped in but it wasn't difficult to find a corner table. Vidyut pulled a chair for Haasini and waited for her to sit down before taking the one opposite.

Haasini couldn't help staring at him, thoroughly impressed by the unexpected chivalry. She had been right in thinking he was a talking-walking temptation to women. Her heart beat rapidly in her chest as she looked at him. "Beer?" she asked, her voice gruff.

He nodded. "Are you allowed to drink?" he asked, tongue firmly in cheek, only to have his arm punched for his effort.

"No more talking about my age, okay? It's not a good conversation to have with a lady," she said firmly, pouting at him.

"With a lady, yes, I agree. But you…?"

"Why don't you go on and finish your sentence?" she said, challenge in her dark gaze, daring him.

He eyed her from the top of her sleek head to her narrow feet encased in red leather strap-on sandals with heels. She was wearing the same outfit she had worn to his office in the morning and looked good enough to eat. The red of her top made her dusky skin glow with health. With just a line of kohl under her eyes and nude gloss on her lips, she looked adorable. "I think I'll pass," he said, giving her a slow grin.

She stared at the dimples which came into play on his slashed cheeks. *Oh my God! He is too hot to handle!* "Are we agreed that I am a lady?" she insisted on asking him.

"Hmm… tell me get back to you on that when we are done with lunch," he said, continuing to tease her mercilessly.

She pouted some more before turning to the waiter and ordering two Hefeweizen beers, pronouncing the word perfectly. "And I would like a plate of the *Naughty Nutties Mix*," she said, before turning to Vidyut with a raised brow.

"*Crispy Aubergine Fry* for me," he said, placing his order for the starter.

Once the waiter left with their order, she asked him, "Are you a fan of brinjal?" wrinkling her nose.

"I love them. I presume you don't?"

She shook her head vigorously. "Never been able to develop a taste for those."

"You must try what they serve here. It's perfectly spiced and fried," he recommended.

She shuddered delicately. "Not for me."

"Have you reviewed this place on your blog?" he asked.

"Yep," she nodded.

"What's the rating?" he asked.

"You have been here before, right?" she answered him with a question of her own.

"Hmm."

"Four stars."

"Kamath's Koffee is truly lucky, I suppose," he grinned. She had given them five stars.

"Not lucky! You guys are too damn good," she said firmly, looking him in the eye. "I mean every word I say in my reviews. That's the reason why I never accept free food."

She took her career seriously! He could see that. And couldn't help but admire her for it. "So, which is your favourite dish at KK's?" he asked, sipping from his bottle of beer.

Taking a sip from her own bottle, she mulled over his question for a minute before saying, "Your mini pizzas are the best! The texture and the choice of toppings are to die for. And I also like your South Indian menu, especially the *Bisibele Bhath*. Truly delicious."

Even as the praise went to his head, Vidyut asked, "I thought the cakes would have won first place."

"They did, before the pizzas happened," she said, grinning at him.

"Aah! I did wonder."

"By the way. I know I told you that I swear by strawberries. But the lemon meringue has become a personal favourite."

He smiled, lifting his half full glass up in a toast. "Thanks."

"Where did you learn to bake so well?" she asked, popping some roasted and spiced nuts into her mouth before pushing the bowl towards him.

"It all began when my mother was trying to teach Avantika how to cook. Avi is my younger sister. She insisted she would learn her way in the kitchen only if I also trained along with her." He laughed. "She was totally against my parents pampering me all because I was a boy."

"Wow! I like your sister, already. And then?"

"So, my mother taught us both to cook. That was the beginning. Later, when I was studying in the US, I had extra time on my hands and a well-equipped kitchen. I began to branch into baking while I made my own meals. And you know how it is! If you enjoy food, you have to perfect the taste while cooking, or it makes you dissatisfied. You know what I mean?"

She nodded. "Oh yes! Even a small pinch of salt can't be more or less. It has to be perfect enough to suit your palate."

"Exactly! Oh yes! Here it is, my favourite aubergine." He eyed the steam raising from the crispy brinjal, relishing the aroma.

She grimaced. "Rather you than me."

"You mean you aren't even going to taste it? Not one li'l bite?" he tempted, tearing off a small piece with his fork before offering it to her. "Go on! Shut your eyes if you want. It will help you savour it all the better. And here, take this tissue. You can spit it out if you don't care for the taste." He was confident that a foodie like her was bound to relish the dish.

Haasini did exactly what he told her to do, shutting her eyes and opening her mouth. She was unable to stop herself from wrinkling her nose when he forked the piece of brinjal into her mouth, a mite scared of closing her lips and chewing on it.

"Be a sport, Haasini! Imagine it's a piece of succulent fish," he urged.

She closed her mouth before letting her tongue feel the flavour and was truly amazed by the texture and taste. It was simply delicious! "Mmm…"

He threw back his head and laughed out loud, feeling triumphant. "So! What's your verdict?" he asked, giving her a naughty grin.

She pulled the plate of fried aubergine over to her side and said, "Order your own!"

"Hahaha!"

Vidyut was surprised to notice it was almost five when they got up from the table after paying the bill.

Time had simply flown in Haasini's company. While she had had three beers, he had refused after the first one.

"But why?"

"I'm driving, aren't I?" he asked logically.

"You follow rules," she uttered the words as if it was a sin, continuing, "I break most rules."

He shrugged. "It's not about rules. It's about common sense. Drunken driving is unsafe. I love myself too much to put my life and limbs at risk."

"Oh!" She had never thought of it like that. "I see."

He grinned. "I'm glad you do."

The conversation between them had flowed comfortably, even the small silences in between, pretty companionable.

"Let me drop you home."

"Thanks."

He didn't take the address, but let her give him directions. About a hundred feet from her bungalow, he frowned, asking her, "Are you related to Haresh Rai by any chance?" It suddenly struck him that her surname was the same as his ex-fiancée's.

She gave him a surprised glance. "Do you know him?" she asked, as always answering his question with one of her own.

He grimaced. "I used to be engaged to his daughter. You have the same surname," he said.

"That's because he's my father. Don't tell me you were engaged to Janani?" asked Haasini, bile rising in her throat.

Vidyut didn't answer immediately as the car swerved out of control and he had to make an extra effort to bring it under control. He stopped it on the left side of the road, diagonally across from Haasini's house.

"I didn't even know she had a younger sister," he declared in a shocked voice. "And I had been engaged to Janani for six whole months."

Horrified, Haasini simply stared at him, rendered completely speechless. The man she was deeply attracted to, the man who made her pulse rate scramble, the man she missed every minute she wasn't in his company—the very same man had been engaged to her sister. That the event was in the past and they weren't engaged any longer was beside the point.

Of all the men in the world, she had to be attracted to her sister's ex-fiancé! Had Vidyut loved Janani? He must have, right? Otherwise, why would they have got engaged? Haasini was truly and completely shaken.

12

Haasini felt sick, even as raw jealousy burned through her innards, turning the food she had consumed, along with the beers, to acid. All the fun they had had during lunch was submerged into nothingness by the new information she had received just now. It made her feel broken.

Shaking her head at him, she said, "I didn't know."

He frowned as he looked in her direction, his gaze unseeing. "That's what I don't understand. Being her sister, how could you not have known that Janani was engaged to me? You didn't attend the ceremony either. Nor did your parents mention they had a younger daughter. Why was that?"

"Did you love Janani a lot?" Haasini followed her own line of thought when she asked the question, her lips drooping at the corners.

"What?" He focused his gaze on her pinched face, wondering what she was talking about. "What did you say?"

"You heard me. Did you love Janani a lot?"

He laughed out loud as if she had cracked a hilarious joke. "Love! There was no love lost between the two of us. It was a purely arranged match. I don't even know why I agreed to the match in the first place. Forgive me, but I don't mean to offend your sister. But my father was insistent I should agree to the "perfect match" as suggested by some friend of his. He didn't give me a choice but to agree. But, wait. You didn't answer my question. How come your parents never mentioned they had another daughter?" His brown gaze was curious now as he looked at her profile even as Haasini turned her face away from him.

She sighed. "I hadn't been living with my parents over the past two years."

"That's no reason for them to hide your very existence." He was genuinely confused. Well, even he had been living abroad for more than four years. But that had never meant his family didn't acknowledge him.

"I presume you aren't engaged to Janani any longer?" She needed to hear it in so many words.

He noticed she didn't reply to his question but was asking another one of her own. Mentally shrugging, he said, "You presume right."

"Why? What happened?"

"Maybe I'll tell you after you tell me why none of your family members mentioned a word about you."

Haasini gave a long sigh which shook her slender form. "It's a long story, Vidyut. I don't think you have either the time or the interest to know the whole of it."

"Why don't you try me?" he suggested, his voice insistent.

"Okay, let me give it to your briefly. I ran away with a guy two years ago and got cut off from my whole family. My parents and sister couldn't face the humiliation and decided to not take my name ever again."

"Oh! But you must have been barely out of school a couple of years ago," he said, his eyes going wide with shock. Deep down, he felt a powerful kick to his solar plexus. She had liked this guy so much that she had been ready to forsake her whole family to go away with him.

"Vidyut!" She shook a fist at him, laughing despite the serious conversation. "I don't know why you keep insisting I am too young to do anything. I was twenty and take full responsibility for my actions. It was not as if Yeshwant lured me away or anything like that. I wanted to be free and I chose to go away with him."

He was liking it less and less. "And?" The Taurus bull mooed loudly.

"And nothing. I realised I didn't really love the man and he had been but a means to an end. Thank God we hadn't got so far as getting married. I left him after three months and made a life for myself in Mysuru."

"And?" The bull's moo was softer this time.

"What? Am I telling you a story or something?" She gave him a mock glare.

He gave her a small smile. "It rather sounds like you are; as if you are talking about someone else's life history."

"Well, there's nothing else to add. I felt a sudden urge to meet my parents and so here I am, back home."

"What did your parents say when you returned?"

"Nothing much. My mom cried a bit. My dad refused to speak to me for a few days. But then, they accepted my presence and things seem alright, as of now."

"No questions asked?"

"No questions asked."

"That's really decent of your folks," he said, all admiration for Haresh and Jyothi Rai who would have become his parents-in-law if Janani had not broken their engagement. He gave a small shudder as he recalled his lucky escape.

"Yeah, I am lucky. Tell me about you and Janani," she said, dying to know all about their relationship.

He shrugged, drawing her eyes to his wide shoulders. "There's nothing to say. There was no Janani and I—not as a couple who could be spoken about in one breath. I got engaged to her because of parental pressure. I insisted that the marriage should take place only after at least one year. We completed six months in July and were thinking of a January wedding. We rarely got to spend time together nor did we chat on the phone." He grimaced. "I used to work with an MNC; sixty-hour weeks. I got sick of it and decided to start my own coffee shop. I never thought I needed my fiancée's or her parents' permission to do so. Tch! She came to the café one day and gave me an ultimatum—that I quit playing with the coffee shop idea and get back to my regular job. I said 'no' and she returned my ring, just like that."

"What?! Are you serious?" Haasini couldn't believe her ears. "Janani gave you the ring just because you changed your career? You both didn't even discuss the matter?"

He gave a bitter laugh. "That was the major problem in our so-called relationship. We never really spoke to each other. The couple of times we met, she always seemed to be in a hurry to get back home; if you know what I mean. Like today, you and I spent four hours at lunch. We chatted some, we laughed some. We know each other a little more than we did yesterday. But… but in the case of my ex-fiancée, I have hardly spoken more than a few sentences with her while she has spoken to me even less."

"Ouch!" That must have been a really bad situation. It was a good thing they weren't engaged any more. But what about Vidyut? His ego must have definitely been hurt. Had the broken engagement spoilt the chances of his having a relationship with some other woman? If that were the case, it would be worse if it was his ex-fiancée's own sister. Why was fate so cruel and twisted?

"But didn't her parents—I mean mine too—have anything to say about it?"

"Your father called mine and told him that the engagement was broken. My dad presumed it was I who had called it off and there was hell to pay. It took me a lot of time and patience to make him see reason. Even then, my dad was insistent it was all my fault as I had thrown away a lucrative job and was putting my time and energy into a risky venture."

She shook her head, lost for words.

Vidyut grinned suddenly. "You know something? Nothing really mattered to me. I may sound selfish, but then, I'd rather be truthful than lie to myself. I wasn't keen on marrying Janani. There was no love lost between the two of us or chemistry for that matter. And neither of us even attempted to become friends. It would have been a complete fiasco. I am just glad we could get out of it before tying the knot."

Haasini gave him an amazed look. Vidyut was being extremely mature and had not really been hurt or upset by Janani's behaviour. "No regrets? Not one little bit?"

"Nope. You must have a clue to the hours I put in at the café. Do you really think I have time for a fiancée or wife?"

As his question was rhetorical, Haasini didn't bother to answer him. Opening the car door, she said, "I'll see you around. We are still on for Wednesday night, aren't we?"

"Of course. Why not?"

She returned his wave before he made a U-turn and went off in the opposite direction.

13

Vidyut made a U-turn and drove on once Haasini got out of his car, his mind working furiously around the strange conversation they had just had. He couldn't wrap his head around the fact that Haasini was Janani's sister.

Oh my God!

Really!

They couldn't be more different than chalk and cheese. Agreed that he didn't know all that much about Janani. Oh yes! He had supposedly known her for more than six months. But he had spoken barely a few sentences to his ex-fiancée, while she had practically ignored him. He shook his head to himself in a daze as he parked the car in front of his café. He hadn't planned to return here as all his work was done. But he was in no state to go home, needing to be alone to think this through.

Haresh and Jyothi Rai had hidden the fact they had a younger daughter who wasn't living with them. All because she had run away from home. How ridiculous was that?! What would have happened if Vidyut and his parents had got to know about it after the marriage?

He shook his head again, walking into the empty café and sitting down on the staircase, holding his head in his hands.

If Haasini had been dead, he could have understood her parents not mentioning her name. But she had been alive all this long. How could they?

As for himself, he had been totally, completely, absolutely, indifferent to Janani—both mentally and physically. As for Haasini, despite their age difference, he was too damn conscious of her—again both mentally and physically. It was incredible how the younger sister aroused such deep feelings in him. And it wasn't even as if they had known each other for long.

Today had been such fun. It had been a joy teasing Haasini, listening to her arguments, to her intelligent conversation. He had thoroughly enjoyed watching her animated face when she chatted with him, having a clear-cut opinion about anything and everything under the sun.

And she worked so hard too; very diligent in her job. At such a young age, she had earned a name for herself in the blogging world; so much so that newspapers sought her articles regarding the hospitality industry. And yes, film reviews too. He truly admired her for it. He had noticed the way she came to his café every morning to work on her laptop.

Vidyut had deliberately kept away from her as he believed she was too young for him. But today, he hadn't been able to refuse her invitation to lunch once she came over personally to his office to invite him. He had even jokingly pointed out the fact that she was way younger than he was. But she didn't seem to care about that.

What the hell! Why should he resist the attraction he felt towards her? That it was powerful was something he couldn't deny. And it looked like she was equally enamoured with him. That was why he had decided to go with the flow and see what happened.

Lunch had been an incredible time spent together and he had been amazed when he realised how the time had flown by before paying the bill; refusing to let her go Dutch. Of course, she had threatened him, insisting she would pick up the tab the next time they went out together. *Haasini might be young in age, but she was definitely mature,* thought Vidyut, a soft smile on his face.

But finding out she was Haresh Rai's daughter and his ex-fiancée's sister had really thrown him for a toss. Talk of it being a small world! It couldn't get any smaller than this, it seemed.

How to deal with the situation now? Vidyut didn't care for the idea of giving up on his budding relationship with Haasini. After all, he had put a lot of thought into it, hesitating to take it further until this morning. The bull-headed Taurus was good at procrastinating, but once he arrived at a decision, it was not easy to wrench him away from it.

It was too bad Janani was Haasini's sister. But that wasn't going to stop Vidyut from getting to know Haasini better. He liked the younger sister and was in fact, captivated by her looks and behaviour. He wasn't going to take a step back at this point. If her family didn't like the idea, it was their lookout.

Finally arriving at that conclusion, he got up to go home. His parents were waiting for him to spend some time with them.

After getting out of Vidyut's car, Haasini's was hesitant as she crossed the road to her bungalow.

She couldn't believe Vidyut had once upon a time been engaged to her sister Janani, of all people in the world! Seriously! Can the world get any smaller than this?

What she failed to understand was how her sister had broken off her engagement with him so easily. Vidyut was handsome, intelligent and such a smart entrepreneur. Why the hell had Janani wanted him to get back to the job he had quit? *Come on, what sense did it make?* Why should he give up something he was keen on doing? Like his coffee shop. And he ran it like a pro too.

Entering her home, Haasini was glad to catch her mother alone on the living room sofa, drinking coffee.

"Mom! Let me join you." Haasini quickly went into the kitchen and made herself some coffee before going to sit with her mother. "Where's Janani?" she asked.

"At a school picnic. She'll return at around eight."

"Good. I wanted to talk to you in private. I heard that Janani had been engaged…" Haasini lifted her brow at her mother, letting the sentence hang in the air.

Jyothi gave a long sigh, the whole of her body shuddering with it. Shaking her head, she said, "He was such a nice boy too. She was engaged to Vidyut Kamath for six months. The marriage was to take place in January.

Just because the boy resigned from his job and planned to start a business, your dad wasn't happy. He told Janani to go and speak to Vidyut, try to persuade him to take his job back and give up the idea of a business. You know how it is *na*, Haasini. Business is very risky and not the same as a job paying a regular monthly salary. But what did Janani do? The stupid girl went and gave him an ultimatum. The boy refused. She immediately removed her ring and returned it to him." She sighed again. "I don't know whether it was her fault or your father's. They are blaming each other. The end result is that we have missed out on a really good match for Janani. Worse than that, we have become the laughing stock of both our extended family and friends. Imagine being engaged for six months and breaking it off only a few months before marriage."

"What is Janani saying?" asked Haasini, curious to know if her sister had any hidden feelings for Vidyut. If that were the case, Haasini would never forgive herself for poaching on Janani's territory.

"Tch! Your sister is a fool. She said that if it wasn't Vidyut, there were a number of other boys who would queue up for her hand. And we could pick and choose any one of them. Even your father had no response to that view. I have given up all hope of finding her a good husband. Let her do whatever she wants." Jyothi ended the story bitterly.

"You don't think she feels something for this Vidyut?"

"How could she? If she had any kind of feeling at all, she wouldn't have broken off the engagement, right? The man has his pride too. Why would he come after her once she has thrown the ring in his face?"

Haasini imagined the scenario—Vidyut chasing Janani with a ring in his hand, hoping to persuade her to wear it again. It simply didn't seem plausible. Vidyut had mentioned he had been relieved when Janani broke off the engagement.

"When did this all happen?"

"Around three months ago. Vidyut was going to inaugurate his café in two weeks. I feel Janani should have been there to support him instead of leaving him like that, high and dry." Jyothi was totally miffed.

Haasini placed a pacifying hand on her mother's shoulder, understanding her angst. But well, she didn't really feel sorry about the scenario. After all, she was half in love with Vidyut herself. She couldn't be gladder that Janani had broken off her engagement to Vidyut. "Don't worry, Mom. Everything happens for the best."

Jyothi gave a reluctant nod, sighing once again. "I suppose you are right. But then, you must understand why I am worried. First, there was this fiasco with you running away from home." Her eyes filled up as Jyothi spoke for the first time about what Haasini had done two years ago. "There was no way I could pacify your father. You know how much he loved... still loves you. Looking back, I can see he was more hurt than angry. But then, anger was the only way he could express himself. And then there was the gossip—our neighbours were relentless..." She raised a hand to stop Haasini when she would have interrupted. "Let me talk, Haasini. Let me get the whole thing off my chest. Where was I? Yes, the neighbours were relentless. After all, Yeshwant was related to the Sharmas and he was a good-for-nothing, according to them. It became difficult for your father and me to go to the temple or the market without being stopped by someone or the other and being questioned. Your Bhavani *atte* has stopped talking to your father from that day. As for the other relatives, they didn't say much to our face, but well, it was obvious they were laughing behind our backs. Your dad blasted me for bringing you up the way I have." She shrugged, pretending to a feeling of nonchalance which she couldn't quite pull off, biting her lip to stop it from trembling with emotion. "It was almost one whole year before things calmed down at home. And then we began looking for a suitable boy for Janani. Things were better when she got engaged to the Kamath boy. They are a respectable family, you know; with only him and a younger sister who's already married to a North Indian."

"Did they know you had another daughter?" asked Haasini, trying to ignore the feeling of heaviness in her chest. After all, she had unwittingly created so much anxiety to her parents.

"How, Haasini? How could we tell them we had another daughter who was way younger than Janani, but who chose to run away from home with a good-for-nothing stranger?" Tears were pouring down Jyothi's cheeks as she looked pathetically at her younger daughter.

"Mom!" Haasini threw her arms around her mother and hugged her tightly. "I'm so sorry, Mom. I didn't think… I didn't realise my running away would create so much unhappiness. I'm truly sorry. I was too self-centred and was only thinking of having fun. Can you please forgive me?"

Jyothi placed both her hands on her younger child's cheeks, reaching forward to kiss her on her forehead. "I was upset and angry only in the beginning. But later, I missed you so much, my dear. Even your father missed you badly. After all, you were only a child. There's nothing to forgive. It was a bad phase in our lives. And now it's all over. I am just grateful my daughter is back with me, unscathed both physically and emotionally."

Haasini buried her face in her mother's shoulder and wept—for her mother, her father and for her foolish younger self.

Haasini decided it was time to bridge the gap between herself and her sister; at least to the level of the uneasy truce they had always shared instead of each of them ignoring the existence of the other. Somehow, they had never been close during the twenty years after Haasini was born. When she returned home after being away for two years, her mother had accepted her immediately. It had taken her father a few days, but he had also come around soon after. But it was Janani who kept her distance till now, not having spoken a single word to her errant sibling.

Haasini waited for her sister to return from the picnic and finish her dinner. Once the parents had retired to their room, she went and sat next to her elder sister who was sitting on the living room sofa, watching a Kannada serial.

"Jan…" Haasini's voice was a quavering whisper. When it had no impact on Janani, she cleared her throat to try once again, "Jan!"

Janani turned to her side with a lifted eyebrow without uttering a word.

"Can't we be friends?" asked Haasini in a pleading voice.

"Why suddenly?" returned Janani in a haughty voice.

Haasini shrugged. "I've been home for two months and…"

"So? I should forgive you for your atrocities?" Janani asked in a stern voice.

"Atrocities? Isn't that coming on a bit too strong?" asked Haasini, holding back her rising temper with difficulty.

"What else will you call your behaviour? Go on. Tell me," Janani challenged, her voice highly sarcastic. She had been biding her time, waiting for the right opportunity to lecture her younger sibling.

"The stupid action of someone too young and ignorant to know what I was doing?" offered Haasini, giving her an appealing glance.

"Stupid, yes. That you most definitely are. Too young I agree. Ignorant? I refuse to accept that. You knew exactly what you were doing when you went away with Yeshwant. You were desperate for sex, that was what you were. And you didn't even care about the shame we— Mom, Dad and I—had to face when everyone spat on our faces." Janani's face was red with pent up anger, her eyes spitting fire at Haasini.

Desperate for sex? Not quite. She had been curious about sex, for sure. And that's why she had run away with Yeshwant. After all, she couldn't just have an affair and get away with it while living under her parents' roof. That was the truth, and Haasini had the guts to accept it—only to herself though. The itch had been scratched and she had found it was no big deal, waking up to her circumstances only too soon. Not one to waste time in regret, she had simply moved out of Yeshwant's home and carried on with her life.

Her only fault was that she had never considered the repercussions of running away in the middle of the night; the impact it would have on her family members and their lives.

Feeling emotional from the time she had chatted with her mother, Haasini teared up on hearing Janani's words. "I'm really sorry, Jan. It was extremely wrong of me to have done what I did. Please forgive me."

Janani jumped up from the sofa, her hands on her hips as she glared at her sister. "Never! Never in this lifetime. I hate you; do you hear me? I just hate you for what you did to Mom and Dad and me. You know what everyone whispered behind our backs? That the younger daughter was in a hurry to get a man, way before the elder one. You left me feeling so damn foolish." She was shouting by now.

Wiping her cheeks with both her hands, Haasini protested, "But… but… listen Jan. I accept I was wrong. But why should they insult you about it? My running away had nothing to do with you." There was a confused scowl on Haasini's face as she tried to wrap her mind around her sister's logic; or rather, the lack of it.

"Oh yeah! Everything is all about you, isn't it? Self-centred bitch!" Janani lifted a hand and slapped her sister hard, on her left cheek. "Why don't you just get lost? My parents might have accepted you. But I will never, ever forgive you for what you did." She swiftly turned away and walked to her room, muttering to herself, "Why were you born at all? I just can't stand you, bitch."

It was a good thing Haasini didn't catch her muttered words, her ears ringing with the impact of the slap she had been dealt. Her whole body shook with anger, her hand trembling as she reached out for the remote control and switched the TV off before taking a bottle of cold water from the fridge and drinking it fully at one go. She wanted to kick herself. Yes! It had been stupid of her to try to pacify Janani who had always disliked her. Why use a mild word such as dislike? It was a fact that her elder sister had always *hated* Haasini.

Her shoulders slouched in defeat, Haasini walked to the balcony, leaning on the railing to stare out into the garden, feeling too deeply hurt by her sister's words as well as her attitude.

Being the Cancer woman she was, family was the foremost for Haasini. She always wanted to surround herself with love and was keen to give love to those around her. But somehow, it had never been possible with Janani. Sigh!

It felt as if Destiny was mocking her. Tch! It was past one before Haasini finally turned to walk to her bedroom. Sleep continued to elude her as she turned this way and that on her bed, feeling too restless.

It was past eleven when she finally woke up in the morning. And for the first time in her career, Haasini had missed a deadline. But just now, feeling the way she did, she didn't give a damn about it.

Vidyut couldn't resist checking out the corner table at his café every hour or so to see if Haasini had come. It was later in the evening when he finally accepted that she wasn't coming.

His lips turning down at the corners in disappointment, he went about his work. Why wasn't she here? Did she have a meeting elsewhere which had kept her away? That must be it. Otherwise, she had been a regular until last Sunday.

Even yesterday, despite it being a holiday for Kamath's Koffee, she had turned up here. That thought finally managed to cheer him. Anyway, tomorrow was another day. And then there was their date at the discotheque.

This time, Vidyut was smiling as he took out the fresh batch of pizzas from the oven.

15

I'll pck u up @ 9. Dnt gt ur car.

Vidyut picked up to check his phone when it pinged at ten on Wednesday morning. He smiled when he saw that the message was from Haasini.

Ok. Bt y nt?

Knowing fully well they would be drinking at the discotheque, he still chose to tease her.

Meh! Pln 2 gt u drnk.

Myb m nt fnd of alchl.

He added a winky emoji to his message.

Vry fny. Ctch u soon.

He laughed when he saw the eye-roll emoji at the end of her message. But where was Haasini? He couldn't help feeling disappointed she might not turn up at the café today either. He stepped out of the kitchen to automatically check out the corner table and grinned when he saw her sitting there in front of her laptop, a mug of coffee next to it.

Walking over quickly, he plonked down on the chair opposite hers before greeting her cheerily. "Hey."

She gave him a sunny smile when she looked up from her laptop. "Hey yourself! How are you?"

He shrugged, studying her face. Was it his imagination or did she look more beautiful than the last time they met? He took in the bright yellow tunic she wore, a string of colourful beads around her neck with matching earrings dangling from her ear lobes. Her hair was rolled up in a chignon on top of her head, a few strands having escaped and caressing her flushed cheeks.

"Have you lost your voice? What did I say?" she asked, sipping from her mug as she gave him a cheeky wink.

He threw back his head and laughed, uncaring when many of the customers turned to look at him. "I'm good. And you?"

She shrugged, her smile disappearing. "Have been better."

"What happened, Haasini?" Had something happened to upset her? Was it the reason she hadn't been to the café yesterday? Vidyut's mind ran in a frenzy as he stared at her, waiting for her answer.

"Tch! Nothing actually." She waved a hand in front of her face, trying to dismiss the torrent of emotions which threatened to bog her down.

"You want to talk? We can go to my office," he offered, not at all liking the idea of her being upset.

She raised her gaze to his, her lips trembling as she tried to control the tears which threatened to fall.

He got up immediately to take her hand. "Come on, let's go." Without waiting for her answer, he pulled her along with him and walked through the kitchen to the back and opened his office cabin with a key. "Sit down," he said, switching on the AC before pulling his phone out to send a message to Nirmal.

Im bsy. Hld frt fr me.

He didn't wait to read Nirmal's reply before going to perch on the corner of his table, close to where Haasini was seated on a visitor's chair. "Tell me."

"Janani hates me," she burst out, silent tears pouring down he face.

"Why do you think so?" asked Vidyut in a shocked voice. He made an effort to keep his face blank, not wanting to upset her more than she already was.

Haasini shook her head, not keen to discuss her conversation with her sister two days ago. "She told me so," Haasini said, her voice a mere whisper.

Vidyut took a couple of deep breaths, wondering how to pacify her. He didn't care for Janani. But she was Haasini's sister and he didn't want to offend Haasini. "Why suddenly?" he asked.

She looked at him through her drenched eyelashes, her pathetic expression squeezing his heart. "I don't think it's all that sudden. She never liked me I think."

"Hmm. Then it shouldn't matter, should it?" he asked, his hands clenched into fists as he controlled his instinct to pull Haasini into his arms.

"It's all fine for you to talk. How would you feel if your sister hated you?" Haasini gave him an accusing look.

Vidyut shook his head. He couldn't imagine Avantika hating him, not under any circumstance. And as for Janani, he was surprised that the cold woman had it in her to feel such a strong emotion such as hatred. "I will be hurt, terribly," he admitted.

Haasini buried her face in her hands, unable to bear the pain of rejection. Even if her sister had not loved her ever, they had at least got along fairly well before. She felt too hurt by this complete alienation.

Unable to see her crying so bitterly, Vidyut jumped off the table and stood next to her for only a second before pulling her out of the chair and into his arms. "No, babe. Don't cry so. I'm sure she's not worth you expending so much of your emotion." He pushed her face into the crook of his shoulder, rubbing her back rhythmically, pressing his chin to the top of her head.

It wasn't long before the sobbing stopped and Haasini wrapped her arms tightly around his lean waist, finding comfort in his hold. She realised that she never wanted to leave his arms. It felt as if she had finally come home.

"Babe?" Vidyut placed a hand on her cheek and lifted her face up to his with his thumb under her chin.

Haasini looked up at him, her eyes wide with wonder as if she was seeing him for the first time. A pulse skittered at her throat, drawing his gaze to it.

Fascinated, he traced a finger over the pulse, excited beyond measure when it beat all the more rapidly. Lifting his chocolatey gaze to hers, he whispered, "Haasini…"

"Vidyut…" Her hand lifted of its own accord to caress his lean cheek, her palm tingling when it came in contact with his skin. "I…" Standing up on her toes, she pressed her mouth to his.

Vidyut groaned, his body going taut with an unexpected hunger, drawing his tongue over the seam of her lips and pushing further in when she opened her mouth invitingly to accommodate him.

Silence reigned in the room for a long time as their kisses turned hotter and deeper, Vidyut leaning back on the table to pull her between his legs, the ache in his groin only increasing by the minute. He didn't seem to get enough of her as he tangled his tongue with hers, excited to feel her equally torrid response.

Finally, they came up for air, Vidyut pressing his forehead to hers, speaking in a hoarse whisper, saying, "What are you doing to me, babe?"

She gave him a wide grin, not bothering to answer as she simply didn't have the strength to utter a single word. It was a while before she could reply coherently. "Not anything different from what you're doing to me, I suppose."

Vidyut rubbed his nose against hers before pressing a kiss to it. Removing her arms from around his lean waist, he stepped back with obvious reluctance. It was all going too fast for the bull. One minute he had been comforting her; and the next they had been locked together in a passionate embrace.

Haasini felt bereft as she stood away from him, her arms hanging at her sides, feeling empty with the warmth of his body denied to her. She lifted her gaze to his, to see if something was wrong. Being extremely sensitive by nature, the crab worried her lower lip, wondering if she had done something to offend him.

"I need to go," he said, not meeting her sharp gaze as he took his buzzing phone from his apron pocket. He quickly began typing with both his thumbs, as if he had completely forgotten her presence.

"Okay." She gave a nod, not even sure if he had noticed it as she was swamped by the depth of what seemed to be his sudden rejection. At least, that's how it appeared to her. For a few minutes, she had simply melted in his arms before he had pushed her away abruptly. What must have gone wrong? She didn't ask the question as her confidence seemed to have deserted her. Making an about turn, she walked out of his cabin, feeling worse than when she had entered it.

Her lips drooping, she sat in her corner of the coffee shop, doing her best to concentrate on her work.

The moment she left his cabin, Vidyut plonked into the chair she had vacated, his head in his hands. What was that all about? Hadn't he told himself she was too young for him? Moreover, Haasini was his ex-fiancée's sister. Okay, it was only the day before yesterday when he had decided that neither Janani nor her parents had a right to interfere if he wanted to get close to Haasini. But now, it felt as if it they were getting too close, too soon. He was quite shaken by the scorching kisses they had shared just now. He still couldn't comprehend how that had come about. One minute he had been pacifying her, drying her tears. The next minute, they had been kissing deeply. Agreed it was she who had made the first move. But what had happened to him? Wasn't he way older than she was? Shouldn't he have had more sense than to takeover and kiss her right back? That too, multiple times?

Vidyut felt like an idiot! And he had promised to go dancing with Haasini in the evening. Considering the state of his aroused body, he couldn't help wondering how he was going to spend a few hours dancing with her at a crowded discotheque.

Sigh! Vidyut made it a point to stay away from Haasini's corner, even though it cost him a lot of effort; completely unaware he was upsetting her more and more.

16

aasini gave a sidelong glance at the silent Vidyut when they entered the discotheque. As promised, she had picked him up at the café at 10.30 PM, not really surprised when she saw him waiting for her, wearing a powder blue linen jacket over his open-collared white shirt paired with dark blue corduroy trousers. His hair brushed back neatly and falling over the collar of his jacket, he looked handsomer than ever.

Vidyut, in turn, didn't miss Haasini's sleeveless dress in hot pink, so short that the skirt stopped at mid-thigh; the matching pink stilettos making her legs appear longer than usual. Long ear-rings dangled from her ears to touch her shoulders while a white sling bag of some shimmering material hung crosswise from her left shoulder to her right hip.

She looked hot, increasing Vidyut's temperature to unbearable levels as he walked a couple of steps behind her when they entered the disco, getting swallowed immediately by the psychedelic lights and thumping music. Conversation was simply not possible for which he was only too grateful.

They walked through the gyrating bodies to reach the bar at the furthest end, Haasini turning around to lift an eyebrow at him.

"Whisky on the rocks," he said, a tad breathless when he noticed her cleavage. For a woman who was almost thin, she had a well-endowed chest. Unable to take his eyes off her luscious breasts, Vidyut took deep breaths, intending to calm down his clamouring libido, without any success.

Haasini turned to the bartender to place their orders. Sipping on her orange cocktail with a dash of gin and white rum, she looked at the dance floor which was crammed to the hilt. Grimacing, she looked at Vidyut who was seated on the barstool next to hers. "What do you think?" she asked.

"About what?" he asked, doing his best to keep his gaze on her gamine face, not missing the high colour on her cheeks and the hot pink lipstick which outlined her soft lips, making them appear sexy.

"The disco, what else?" she responded, a tad sarcastically. He hadn't been his usual self after the kisses they had shared in his office. Dammit! It took two, didn't it? Why the hell was he angry with her?

He shrugged, drawing her gaze to his broad shoulders. "Looks good."

"And you look good enough to eat." Haasini reached across to speak into his ear, uttering the words slowly and clearly, making sure he heard them. She grinned when she saw the rush of heat on his slashed cheeks.

"Haasini..."

"What?" Her eyes danced even as she raised an eyebrow in enquiry.

"Are you flirting with me?" he asked, his chocolatey gaze serious.

"What if I am?" she challenged, tilting her glass to finish off her drink before ordering a second one.

"Are you sure you are prepared for the repercussions?" he asked loudly, refusing to move closer to speak into her ear, the way she had done.

"Try me." She jumped off her stool and lifted her hand, palm up in front of him. "Dance?"

Gulping down the last of the whisky in his glass, Vidyut slipped off his stool and took her hand before they joined the crowd, swinging in tune to the music. Soon, he forgot his discomfort and enjoyed himself as they danced to every number—fast and slow—the DJ churned out.

"Time out please," groaned Haasini after an hour, taking his hand in hers to walk to the bar. "I'm parched."

He grinned, taking her second drink—the bartender had made before they went dancing—and handing it to her. Not stopping to think, he placed his hands on her slim waist to lift her on to a barstool, giving her a startled glance when he heard her squeak. "What's wrong?" he asked solicitously.

She shook her head, her eyes on his face. He had lifted her as if she was as light as a feather. She might be thin, but Haasini knew that she carried a good weight. So! All that muscle he sported was not just for show. They were also an indicator of inherent strength. "Nothing," she said in a breathless voice.

Settling on the stool next to her, he asked for another whisky, with soda and ice this time. "Do you want to get something to eat?" he asked her, whispering into her ear, his lips brushing over the shape.

Her ear tingling with awareness, she gave him a small nod. "Shall we move to the dining area?"

"I suppose." He got off his stool to stand next to her, waiting patiently while she paid for their drinks. Just when she returned her card to her sling bag, he lifted her again before standing her on the floor.

She gazed up into his eyes, wondering at his behaviour. He had been so cold on their way here. But now, he was blowing hot, lifting her on to the stool and now off it. What game was he playing?

"Let's go." He took her hand in his as he drew her towards the dining room, giving an exaggerated sigh of relief at the silence which greeted them. The head waiter guided them to a corner table for four before handing them the drink and food menus.

"I'm famished," declared Haasini as she opened the food menu.

"Hmm… I'll have another whisky with soda and the mutton kababs," said Vidyut, reading the menu in her hand from the opposite side.

"Can you read upside down?" she asked, giving him a startled glance.

"Can't everyone do that?" he asked, puzzled. He didn't believe it was some exceptional skill.

"Of course not. I can't, for one."

"Have you actually tried it?" he asked, opening the drinks menu. "Go on, try this one."

She gaped at him for a few seconds before turning her gaze to the menu in his hand. It took her a couple of minutes to adjust before she read the names of the premium whiskies on offer before laughing out loud. "That was too damn easy."

"Exactly." He grinned, his gaze rivetted to her laughing face, finding her too fascinating for words. The fact was he was deeply attracted to her—both her beautiful body and her intelligent mind. And somehow, he was convinced that she returned his feelings. Was it enough for a long-term relationship? His mind turning to the time she had spent away from home, he wondered about the man she had run away with. "Haasini, were you in love with Yeshwant?"

"Huh?" It was a whole minute before Haasini realised Vidyut was talking about something else altogether. It took her a few more seconds to recall who Yeshwant was. It also surprised her that Vidyut remembered the name she had mentioned but once. "Why do you ask?"

He shrugged. "Just! Are you going to answer my question?" His brown gaze bored into her deep, black one. He turned to the waiter impatiently when the man walked over to take their order.

Haasini quickly told the waiter what they wanted and waited for the man to leave before giving Vidyut her whole attention. She wasn't sure why he wanted to know about Yeshwant. But it was better she told Vidyut everything if she wanted to take their relationship to the next level.

"I was barely twenty. That's no excuse," she said, lifting a hand to stop him when Vidyut would have interrupted. "It's just that I wasn't high on intelligence or maturity. My parents are conservative. There's nothing wrong with that. But for a rebel like me, there was this need to live a life outside their line of control, if you know what I mean. They weren't all that strict. But what's the fun in reporting every movement of mine? Informing them of every minute I spent outside home? I wanted to have fun. And for me, fun was in living an independent life away from them. A simpler way would have probably been to shift to a different city to complete my education. But I didn't want to study beyond my BA."

She paused to sip on her cocktail before continuing, "Yeshwant Sharma came to stay with his cousin next door. Twelve years older than me, he was the epitome of maturity. I was floored that an older man as attractive as he, was interested in me." She grimaced. "Please don't ask me why I thought he was attractive." She shuddered, recalling the time when she had concluded his appearance was but a façade. "It didn't take all that long to open my eyes; see through the fake gloss he had been projecting. He had dropped out of college and had no family. He lived in a rental flat in Mysuru, doing odd jobs to make enough money to survive. He had no purpose in life. No drive." And for the Cancer woman that was a huge minus in her partner. "Ugh! While I was looking for adventure, he was out for someone who would serve him twenty-four-seven and that too free of cost."

"Ouch!" Vidyut took her slender hand in both of his. "You were so young." His heart went out to the younger Haasini, even as he felt jealousy and anger churn within him at the unknown Yeshwant Sharma.

Haasini shook her head, giving him a wide smile. "Don't underestimate me. It wasn't as if Yeshwant fooled me; at least not for long. Nor was it as if he was like a stone tied around my neck. I went into the relationship with my eyes open. I used him as much as he used me. Once I realised he wasn't the man I thought he was, I simply left him."

Vidyut's jaw dropped. "You did what?"

"You heard me," she said, grinning wickedly. "I suppose my relationship with Yeshwant was something similar to yours with Janani. There was no emotion involved; just a means to an end."

He couldn't have put it in better and more succinct words. She had summed it all up so beautifully. "You lived with him." Vidyut couldn't stop the trace of jealousy which continued to dog him.

"Yep. For three months." Her voice was matter-of-fact.

"Did you love him?" Vidyut was right back at square one, wanting to know the level of her emotional involvement with her ex.

Haasini wrinkled her nose at him. "What is love? If by that you mean the need to stay put with someone come hell or highwater, then…" she shook her head, "… I never loved him."

A slow smile spread across Vidyut's face, bringing his fascinating dimples into play. He gave a small nod of understanding. "I know what you mean." Did it also mean he was in love with Haasini? He felt a deep urge to be with her forever. His throat choking with emotion, he simply stared at her lovely face. How had it happened? And when? Had he fallen in love with her the day he sets eyes on her? Or had Haasini grown on him little by little?

Whatever it was, Vidyut realised that he wanted her to be a permanent part of his life. Will she agree? More than all that, did she return at least a small portion of his feelings?

It was Haasini's turn to stare at Vidyut. *Does he know what I mean?* It was the truth she hadn't felt anything towards Yeshwant; not even a hundredth of what she felt for Vidyut now. And yes! She felt a powerful need to stay by Vidyut's side, come hell or highwater. But what about him? Did he feel for her even an iota of the feelings she had for him?

"Haasini…" Vidyut dropped the fork with a clatter before taking her hand once again in his. "I…"

She gulped down the drink, almost choking as it went down the wrong way. Spluttering, she gave him a mock glare, an eyebrow raised. Her throat felt too raw for her to be able to utter a single word.

Taking a deep breath, he bent his head to press his mouth to the back of her hand, even as he pinned her with his brown gaze. "I think I'm falling in love with you."

Curling her fingers over his hand, she gave him a small nod, still unable to get a sound out through her vocal cords. They seemed to have abandoned her.

"Don't tell me you are lost for words! I refuse to believe it." While he teased her, he was quaking from within. It wasn't simple, hanging his heart on his sleeve and waiting for her to respond in kind.

Haasini got up from her sofa and went over to sit next to him, burying her face in his chest. "Hold me," she croaked, on the verge of tears. She was dazed that a man like Vidyut—so handsome and a successful entrepreneur too—was falling in love with her. She had wished; she had hoped. But she hadn't expected him to return her feelings; not by a long shot.

Vidyut pulled her into his lap, his arms going around her waist and her back pressed to his chest. "With pleasure, babe," he growled, kissing the crook of her neck and shoulder.

Her nerves stretched taut with longing, Haasini turned her head to press her lips to his rough cheek. "I want you."

He lifted his head to look at her blushing face. "You lust me."

"I do," she said, looking deeply into his eyes. "Do you have a problem with that?"

He shook his head, giving her a slow grin which made her blood zing. "Not at all. Have you eaten all you want?"

"Not really. It's you I want for dessert."

He threw back his head and laughed, pushing her off his lap to signal the waiter for the bill.

She pouted at him, trying to climb into his lap once again.

"Let's go now. I want you all to myself," he growled, kissing her jawline.

Once their cab left them outside Kamath's Koffee, Vidyut took Haasini's hand and helped her out before walking towards the back entrance. Opening the door which led into the kitchen, he drew her to the back staircase that led them to the space above his office cabin on the ground floor.

He opened the door with another key and Haasini's jaw dropped when she saw the bedroom beyond. It was the ultimate in luxury. "Is this your bachelor's pad?" she asked in an awed whisper.

"If, by that you mean if I bring my girlfriends here, then no. The few nights I have slept here, I have always been alone." His voice was gruff as he drew her into the room and shut the door behind them.

Haasini was touched by his words—by his honesty and the fact that she was the first woman he had brought here. And she hoped to be the last.

"Haasini…" He pulled her into his arms, nuzzling her neck, his mouth seeking the pulse which beat erratically there.

"Vidyut!" Throwing her arms around his neck, she stepped closer, tilting her head to accommodate his feverish kisses along her neck and shoulder. She protested loudly when he removed her arms from around his neck and stepped away.

"Just a minute, babe." He quickly discarded his linen jacket before unbuttoning his shirt, smiling when Haasini pushed his hands away to take over the task.

Her eyes went wide as she took in Vidyut's bare chest sprinkled with hair, even as she pushed the shirt off his shoulders. "You look gorgeous," she uttered in a whisper before reaching forward to kiss him in the centre of his chest.

Ignoring the heat and colour rushing up his lean cheeks, he curled his fingers into the shoulder straps of her dress, asking, "May I?"

Haasini turned around to draw his attention to the zip at the back which held her dress in place.

He quickly pulled the zip down, pushing the straps down her arms before wrapping his arms around her slender waist, his face buried in the crook of her shoulder. "You are beautiful, babe." He removed the hook of her bra before turning her around.

Instinctively, Haasini crossed her arms over her chest, gazing up at him warily. She had simply hated it when Yeshwant had touched her breasts roughly, his hands hard when he squeezed them mercilessly.

"I wanna see you," said Vidyut in a gruff whisper, looking deeply into her eyes.

Unable to refuse him, she uncrossed her arms before pulling the scrap of lace which covered her breasts.

Vidyut drew in a deep breath as his wide gaze took in her twin mounds. Luscious! That's what she was. "Gorgeous," he declared, going on his knees in front of her, cupping the undersides of both breasts in his hands.

Haasini shut her eyes tightly, waiting for the feeling of revulsion to sweep her; only to gasp when she felt the lightest of touches as he brushed his thumbs across the tips of her breasts. Opening her eyes, she stared at his intent face as he circled her nipples over and over with his thumbs.

Moving his gaze from her breasts to her face, he smiled, asking, "Do you like it?"

She gulped, giving him a small nod. "Yes!"

He bent his head to kiss the top of one breast before running his damp tongue in an arc just above the aureole.

"Vidyut..." She was panting by now, her hands clutching his head and pulling him closer to her breasts.

He smiled, his left hand cupping her right breast gently even as he caressed her left breast with his lips and tongue.

She dug her hands into his scalp, a kind of desperation driving her as she wanted him to kiss the tip. Only he refused to oblige even as he traced his tongue round and round the aureole. "Vidyut!" Her voice was commanding as she glared down at his dark head.

"What is it, babe?" he asked, moving away just enough to look up at her face, his eyes slumberous with desire.

"Please..."

"Please what?" he asked, giving her a naughty grin. "Don't you like my loving your breasts?" he asked, squeezing her right breast gently, even as he rubbed his thumb over the sensitive tip.

She shook her head before nodding, making him laugh out loud. How to tell him that she wanted him to take her nipple in his mouth? She was confident by now that he wouldn't hurt her; not like Yeshwant had. "I want you to…"

"You want me to…?" he asked.

"You know what I want," she said, aching to feel his mouth on her.

Hearing the longing in her voice, he reached forward to stroke the tip of her breast with his tongue. "Is this what you want?" he asked, looking up at her once again.

Haasini moaned, eager for more. "I wanna more…"

He reached out to stroke her with his tongue once again before closing his mouth over the tip, drawing the nipple deep into the warmth of his mouth. Soon, he was suckling her breast, thrilled to hear her mewling in pleasure. It wasn't long before he removed his caressing hand from her other breast and turned his head to lave it with his tongue.

"Yes…" Haasini was trembling with desire and excitement when the heat of his mouth enclosed the sensitive tip of her breast. Taking his hand, she placed it over her still damp left breast, rubbing herself into his palm. A sudden tremor shook her body when she felt his other hand cup the mound of her femininity. "Vidyut…"

He stood up to lift her into his arms and carry her to the king-sized bed before laying her down gently as if she was the most precious bundle, before lying down next to her. Cupping her face in his palms, he kissed her on her mouth, his tongue duelling with hers.

Haasini ran her hands feverishly down his smooth back, revelling in the velvety texture which encased the steel of his muscles. When her hands encountered the waistband of his pants, she protested loudly.

Totally lost in nibbling her collar bone, a startled Vidyut moved away to ask, "What?"

"You still have your pants on," she grumbled, reaching forward to bite his lower lip.

"My mistake," he growled, pressing a hard kiss to her lips before getting up from the bed to unbuckle his belt ands removing his pants.

Haasini stared at him; first his chest and then his muscular thighs which came into view. Her gaze stopped at the tumescent bulge tenting his briefs. Unable to resist, she reached a hand to touch him, delighted to hear him groan. She cupped him through the briefs, caressing his length.

"Temptress!" He chucked his pants even as he pressed himself into her hand. "Want to help me remove these?" he asked, pointing to his briefs.

She knelt on the bed, her tongue peeping between her teeth as she concentrated on the task. Tucking her thumbs into the sides, she pulled his briefs down, her dark, fascinated gaze on the length of his penis. Oh my God! He was simply fantastic. She drew in a deep breath before it came out in a loud gasp. She curled her left hand around him, caressing him with her right hand, drawing it from the root to the tip. She rubbed her thumb over the tip and smiled when it came away with a drop of moisture.

"Haasini…" He gulped when she leaned forward to run her tongue over the path her hand had taken, his hands holding her head even as she closed her mouth over the tip of his penis, sucking on it gently. He groaned long and loud before pushing her back on the bed. He lifted her legs to draw them around his lean waist. Just when he would have entered her, he stopped suddenly, snarling, "Damn it!"

"What?" Haasini's hands were on his shoulders before she ran them down his arms, taking pleasure in caressing the strong biceps. "Why did you stop?"

"I don't have condoms. Shit!" He moved away from her to stand at the side of the bed. "I'm sorry," he muttered, feeling utterly foolish.

She jumped off the bed to pick up her sling bag which had fallen on the floor. Opening it, she handed him two foil packets. "Here you go."

"Haasini! You... I..." He didn't know if he should feel relieved or bugged that she was walking around with condoms in her bag.

"What? Is it only a man's job?" she asked challengingly.

He grinned suddenly, taking the packets from her hand and tearing one open. His hands trembled when he pulled it over his manhood. Turning to her, he pulled her into his arms, kissing her hard even as he tumbled her on the bed. "You are a life saviour," he declared before entering her in one stroke.

Her giggle turned to a loud moan when she felt him fill up her slick core, locking her legs around his lean waist; even as she caressed his chest with her hands, her thumbs rubbing over his flat nipples.

Vidyut pumped into her, forgetting to be gentle when he heard her moans grow louder and louder, his hands on her breasts as he tweaked the tips with his thumbs and forefingers.

Haasini lifted her head to capture his mouth in a passionate kiss, drawing his tongue deeply into her mouth, even as she felt an unfamiliar pressure build in her womb. She shook her head, clinging to Vidyut's shoulders as the pressure increased manifold, driving her crazy as she tried to grab something which was constantly out of reach.

Oh my God! What was happening to her? Goaded beyond endurance when Vidyut pumped into her repeatedly, she sunk her teeth into his shoulder, wondering if she would ever feel normal again. She seemed to have lost control of her body as she met him thrust for thrust, still unable to fathom where this was going.

And suddenly it happened! A flood of sensation which shattered her nerves to shreds even as it felt as if her body had rocketed into space, feeling so light as she floated among the stars.

It was Vidyut's long groan of satisfaction which brought her back down to earth, Haasini finally being able to feel her body. She gathered him in her trembling arms, burying her face in his chest, uncaring of the tears flowing down the sides of her face.

Vidyut flopped down on the bed beside her, thrilled beyond measure that she was holding him so close; his throbbing shoulder giving him proof of Haasini's passionate nature.

"Are you okay?" he whispered into her ear, a hand cupping her breast tenderly.

She turned to give him a dazzling grin. "Ne'er been better."

"I love you, babe!"

"Tell me again," she ordered, a finger tracing the shape of the dimple on his cheek.

"I love you, Haasini."

"You know something? I think I fell in love with you when I saw your dimples come into play."

"So, it wasn't me, but my dimples," he teased.

She poked her tongue at him. "That simply means you should smile always."

"Aah!" He turned her around, spooning her body to his and hugging her close, his hand continuing to fondle her breasts. "I can't seem to get enough of your breasts. Hope you don't mind."

She placed a hand over his, pressing it closer to her breast. "Mind? Never! I love your hands on my breasts."

"And my mouth?" he asked.

She turned around to pull his head to her chest. "I love it even more..." She moaned when he closed his mouth over a nipple and suckled it; before their passionate lovemaking began all over again.

18

Arun opened his laptop to work on the accounts of Kamath's Koffee, thrilled beyond measure when he noted that the daily turnaround had been steady throughout the month. Vidyut's business was doing very well and he felt so proud of his son.

More than all that, Arun was happy for himself; that he had a useful occupation. Retirement hadn't suited him at all. With too much time on his hands, he tended to get bored, irritating his wife in the process.

Now, though he went to his son's café only three or four days in a week, that too only for a few hours, it was enough to make him feel useful. And Arun knew for a fact that his handling the accounts left Vidyut with more time to manage the café. Both father and son were happy with the arrangement.

It was Monday and Vidyut was out, arranging for some much-needed supplies while Arun worked on the accounts. He looked up when he heard the door open, wondering who it could be.

"Good morning, Vidu!" Haasini pushed open the office door and stepped into it.

"Hello! Vidu isn't here," said Arun, staring dumbfounded at the beautiful young woman who had stepped into his son's office without so much as a by-your-leave.

With a lot of effort, she managed to shut her dropping jaw and stared at the man who was seated in Vidyut's office chair, wondering if Vidyut would look like him after a few decades.

"Hello Uncle. Are you Vidyut's father?" she asked outright, stepping closer to the table.

"That's right. You have the advantage of me, young lady. I don't know who you are."

She brought both her hands together in a respectful greeting. "I am Haasini Rai, Arun Uncle. I…"

Arun sat back in his chair as if preparing for a long chat. "Are you the one who wrote the article about Kamath's Koffee in Bengaluru Express?" He was doing his best to fathom her relationship with Vidyut. After all, she hadn't even bothered to knock on the door before entering. He concluded she must know his son well.

Haasini smiled broadly. "You are right, Uncle; it was I who wrote the piece. I hope you liked it."

"It was an excellent article, Haasini. Why don't you sit down? I'll ask Nirmal to get us something to drink. Coffee? Or do you prefer tea?"

"I like coffee. And I've already messaged Nirmal to get two cups over to the office. I hope you don't mind."

She didn't lack for confidence. That was for sure. And Arun could see that she was truly beautiful. Was she a bit too young for Vidyut? The father couldn't help thinking in terms of getting his son married off. After all, it was more than three months after his engagement was broken. "Not at all, my dear. So, what else do you write?"

Haasini chatted comfortably with him, telling him of her blog and the reviews she covered for mainstream media.

Nirmal knocked on the door and brought in a tray with coffee and cookies. "Hi Nirmal," greeted Haasini, giving him a wave.

"Hello, ma'am. How are you?"

"I'm good. Thanks for the coffee."

"Anytime, ma'am." Turning to Arun, he asked, "Do you need anything else, sir?" When Arun shook his head, Nirmal took his leave and went.

So! Haasini was a regular at Vidyut's coffee shop. Nirmal treated her like a familiar face. Arun took a mug and sipped from it.

"Where's Vidyut, Uncle?" Haasini blew on the coffee before taking a small sip.

"He's visiting a supplier." Arun looked at the wall clock behind Haasini before saying, "He should be back in half an hour or so."

"Oh!" She finished the coffee and wondered what to do. "I'll take myself off then. Thanks for the coffee, Uncle."

"Why don't you wait for him?"

"Won't I be disturbing you?" she asked. She wouldn't really mind chatting with Arun Kamath. Vidyut's father seemed so nice.

"Not at all, my child. Why don't you tell me more about yourself and your family? And here, have some cookies."

"Thank you, Uncle." Haasini helped herself to a chocolate chip cookie.

In the next half an hour, they had become the best of friends, Haasini speaking a lot about her work and her ambitions. She also asked a number of questions about Vidyut and Arun himself.

A few minutes into the conversation, Arun realised that she was Janani Rai's sister. He had a difficult time not to frown. How strange was this situation?! But then, he didn't want to delve too much into it—not until he was sure about Vidyut's and Haasini's relationship.

But then, how come Haresh Rai had never mentioned he had a younger daughter? It was so odd. Arun decided to tackle Vidyut regarding the matter.

"I was surprised when I got to know that Vidyut cooks so well. Indian boys generally don't…"

Arun laughed. "You are right. Generally, Indian boys don't enter the kitchen or do any household work. Take me, for instance. I don't lift a finger at home. Poor Vandana manages everything. But then, your generation is different. My daughter, Avantika, for example—she put her foot down and insisted she won't do any work at home unless Vandana trained Vidyut to do housework as well." He laughed again, reminiscent of those times.

"In the beginning, Vidyut resisted. He was, what? Fourteen years, I think. Avantika was eleven. A typical teenage boy, he was into cycling, basketball, and video games. While Vandana was keen that Avantika should learn the ropes of housekeeping. There was hell to pay, I believe. I was busy at work. But my daughter threw tantrums until Vidyut agreed to work along with her." There was a reminiscent smile on his face.

Haasini laughed softly. "I agree with your daughter, Uncle. I have only a sister and we were treated the same;

more or less. But I can understand where Avantika must come from."

"Why don't you come home with us for lunch once Vidyut returns?" asked Arun suddenly. He was keen that Vandana should meet Haasini too. The girl was too sweet and he felt she would make Vidyut a perfect partner.

Colour bloomed on Haasini's face when she heard Arun's words. "Are you sure, Uncle?"

"Of course I am. Unless you don't want to?" He gave her a sly glance.

Haasini laughed. "I would love to go, Uncle."

"Where are you guys planning to go?" asked Vidyut, walking into the office. He had entered the cabin a couple of minutes ago, but neither his father nor his girlfriend had been aware of his presence. And it looked like the two of them were getting along like a house on fire. Not bad!

She turned around when she heard Vidyut's voice and gave him a broad smile, saying, "Hi."

Arun said, "Haasini came looking for you. I persuaded her to spend some time with me. And now she'll be coming home with us for lunch."

All in one afternoon! Not bad at all. Vidyut went to sit next to her, giving her a wink before turning to his father. "Are you sure she wasn't troubling you, *Appa*?" he asked mischievously.

"Don't be silly, Vidu. It was a pleasure chatting with Haasini. Shall we go home for lunch? Or do you need to finish something else before we leave?"

Haasini's head turned in a flash, a shocked expression in her eyes as she stared at Vidyut's profile. Uncaring that his father was sitting across the desk, he was caressing her thigh which was closest to him, making her blood sizzle with desire.

"Nothing, *Appa*. We can leave. Is either of you going to have that cookie?" he asked, pointing to the plate with his chin.

"Not for me," said Arun, pushing the plate towards his son.

"Haasini?" Vidyut turned to gaze at her, his eyes the colour of molten chocolate as he studied her red face. "You want to share?"

Too choked to speak, she gave him a nod before breaking the cookie in two. She gave him an intense glare when he would have leaned forward to take the piece in her hand directly into his mouth.

With a wicked smile, he picked the other half from the plate and shoved it into his mouth. "Just two minutes, *Appa*. Nirmal is getting me a cup of coffee."

His father nodded, shutting the laptop after making sure that all the files he had been working on were saved. He was unaware of the byplay going on right under his nose.

Haasini gasped when she felt Vidyut's hand moving towards her groin. Intending to stop its progress further, she clamped her thighs together, inadvertently trapping his hand against her vagina. She lifted her shocked gaze to his only to find him grinning naughtily at her.

Jumping to her feet, Haasini said, "If you'll both excuse me, I need to make a call." Without waiting for a reply from either of them, she stepped out of the cabin, waving to Nirmal as he carried a mug of coffee inside.

Vidyut thanked Nirmal and instructed him to lock up when he heard his phone ping. Checking the messages, he bit his lip to stop himself from laughing out loud. The message was from Haasini.

I'll gt u fr ths

He quickly typed a reply

Cnt wt

Meh

"Vidu, you do know Haasini is Janani's younger sister, don't you?" asked Arun once Nirmal left the office cabin.

"Yes, *Appa*. I got to know only last week."

"Er… what…?" Arun hesitated. How could he ask his grownup son if he was interested in a woman?

"You want to know about my relationship with Haasini, right?"

Arun nodded; his face serious.

"I like her a lot, *Appa*. I was going to bring her home next month and introduce her to you and *Amma*. I would like to marry her with both your blessings." Vidyut drank his coffee, looking at his father.

Arun sighed, a worried frown on his face. "I like Haasini too. But how are her parents going to take this news? And they might want their elder daughter married before getting the younger one tied up."

Vidyut nodded. "I am in no hurry, *Appa*. Haasini is very young. I…"

"I noticed that. And that's another thing I wanted to speak to you about. Haresh Rai never mentioned having a younger daughter. Isn't that surprising?"

"Very surprising." He got up from his chair, waiting for his father to get up as well. "Let's go have lunch. We can talk in the evening."

Catching on that his son didn't want to discuss the matter with Haasini around, Arun gave a nod as he walked out of the cabin along with Vidyut.

Haasini had been talking to her mother, explaining that she will not be home for lunch when she caught sight of the father-son duo. "I'll catch you later, Mom," she said, disconnecting the call. "Are we ready to go, Uncle?" she asked, looking at Arun as she studiously ignored Vidyut who was trying to catch her eye.

"Yes, Haasini. So, what kind of food do you like?" asked Arun, walking at her side.

Haasini almost jumped when she felt Vidyut's hand on her bottom as he cupped it. She couldn't even react with his father around. What the hell was he trying? Before she could move away, she felt him pinch her soft flesh, just for a second before his hand was removed.

"I... uh... I like almost all kinds of food, Uncle."

"Is there something you don't like?" Arun didn't notice Haasini stuttering when she answered him.

"I used to dislike brinjal. But I have started liking it too nowadays," said Haasini, getting into the back seat of the car when Vidyut opened the door for her. "What are you trying?" she growled at him just as Arun opened the car from the front.

Vidyut gave her an innocent glance. "I? Why do you ask? I don't..."

She slapped his straying hand when he tried to touch her breast, before pushing him out of the way and shutting the car door in his face. Watching Arun as he settled down in the front passenger seat, she quickly poked her tongue at Vidyut before sitting back in her seat.

A laughing Vidyut got into the driver's seat and pulled the seatbelt across himself before locking it in place. He shifted the rear-view mirror so that he could watch her, giving her a quick wink before gunning the engine.

Her face hot with rushing colour, Haasini turned her head to stare out of the window, waiting for an opportunity to get back at her boyfriend who was projecting a totally naughty side of himself today. Her whole body tingled with awareness as she recalled his touch on her thigh and later, on her bottom. She flashed a look at the rear-view mirror to meet his twinkling glance for just a second before turning to the window again.

"Do you cook, Haasini?" asked Arun, turning his head to look at her.

"Like a pro, Uncle. I worked as a cook for the guests at a homestay in Mysuru for a couple of years."

"Really?! That must have been for a lot of people." He turned to give her an astounded glance. She looked so young. "How old are you? If you don't mind my asking."

Vidyut guffawed, much to Haasini's irritation.

"I don't see anything funny," said Arun, turning to glare at his son.

"Exactly. I don't see anything funny either," agreed Haasini before answering Arun, "I am twenty-two, Uncle."

"And you had been cooking at that homestay for two years. You must be good."

"Why don't you ask her if any of the guests ever returned after their first stay, *Appa*?" inserted Vidyut, his tongue firmly in cheek.

Haasini's gaze promised him murder through the rear-view mirror before she focused her attention on the father. "I am really good at cooking, Uncle. You please don't listen to Vidyut."

"I won't, my dear. Vidyut, why don't you keep quiet and concentrate on getting us all safely home while I chat with this delightful young lady?" Arun shut his son up effectively before continuing to converse with Haasini.

Vandana opened the door when the bell rang, her curious eyes falling on the strange girl who had accompanied her son and husband home.

"Vandana, this is Vidyut's friend Haasini. And Haasini, this is Vidyut's mother." Arun performed the introductions as soon as they entered the living room.

"Hello, Vandana Aunty!" Haasini brought her hands together in a respectful greeting, smiling at Vidyut's mother.

Vandana turned from one man to the other before returning her gaze to the guest. "Hello Haasini! Welcome to our home."

"Do you remember the article about Kamath's Koffee which was published in Bengaluru Express? It was Haasini who wrote it." Arun explained to his wife.

A wide smile stretched across Vandana's face. "You are *that* Haasini. Lovely meeting you, my dear. Come along in and sit down."

Vidyut kept standing while the other three sat down. After a couple of minutes, he said, "Can we have lunch? I'm hungry."

"Yes, yes. Everything's ready. Let me..."

"You don't get up, *Amma*. I'll bring the food."

"I can help you," said Haasini, jumping to her feet immediately, impressing the older couple even more.

Vandana felt torn between excitement and exasperation when her husband told her on an aside that the visiting young lady was also Vidyut's girlfriend. Both Vidyut and Haasini were still in the kitchen, warming the food before bringing it to the dining table.

"I think she's perfect for our Vidu. What do you say?" asked Arun.

Vandana snorted. "Did you ask your son first? Yours and my opinions won't count if he doesn't like her."

Arun gave his wife a startled glance. Vandana always sided with her son. He was surprised that she sounded angry just now. "Is something the matter?" he asked her.

Vandana sniffed. "All my friends are curious about why Vidu's engagement was broken. I tried telling them that the astrologer told us much later that Vidyut and Janani were not really suited. But I have a strong feeling they didn't really believe me."

Arun stared at his wife askance. "But why tell them a lie?" he asked, a small frown pleating his forehead.

"Then what should I tell them? That Janani and her parents had decided that our son wasn't good enough for them?" Vandana glared at her husband.

"You have a point there." Arun sighed. "Anyway, that's no reason for you to be angry with Vidu. It's not really his fault the engagement was broken. Our son is handsome and intelligent. I suppose that Janani wasn't good enough for him. But this girl, Haasini, I tell you, I had a long chat with her when Vidyut was out. She is perfect for him." He refrained from telling his wife that Haasini was actually Janani's younger sister. He felt it was better to get across one point at a time, without shocking his wife all at one go.

In the meanwhile…

Vidyut walked ahead into the kitchen, Haasini following him close behind. Just as he switched on the gas, she placed her hands on his shoulders before going on tiptoe to take a sharp nip of his earlobe.

"Ouch! That hurt!" he grumbled, turning to grab her in his arms.

"Terribly, I hope," she growled, nipping his lower lip even harder.

"You she-cat!" he growled, taking her mouth in a torrid kiss. "Did I tell you how cute you look when you're in a temper?" he asked, tracing the line of her jaw with his lips.

"Meh! That was mean, Vidyut. How could you touch me so intimately with your father sitting right across from us?"

He laughed softly. "Wasn't it fun?" he asked, giving her a wink.

She pouted at him, unable to help but see his point. Smiling widely, she pulled his head down to kiss him. Taking his hand, she placed it on her breast. "I love it when you touch me." She heaved a deep sigh of pleasure when he squeezed her breast. "But then, I want to fuck you immediately. You do realise what could have happened, don't you?"

He tilted his head back to gaze into her stormy gaze. "You would have really fucked me? With my father around? Now this I must see."

Haasini stamped his foot, hard; cackling joyfully when he yelled in pain. "Serve you right!" Tilting her chin, she quickly transferred the steaming *tomato rasam* from the sauce pan into a steel bowl and walked out of the kitchen with the container.

Vidyut shook with laughter as he removed the *mosaru bajji*—chopped salad veggies tossed in beaten curd along with chopped green chillies and coriander leaves—from the fridge and the *chicken biryani* from the cooker where it was keeping warm before carrying them out to the dining table.

"I fried some *papads*," called out Vandana.

"I'll get them," said Vidyut, turning to Haasini, "Do you want to bring the plates?" He lifted a lazy eyebrow at her, his chocolatey eyes promising retaliation.

Her heart thudding with excitement, she gave him a nod before following him, thrilled when he turned around to kiss her once again, duelling her tongue with his.

"I can't seem to keep my hands off you," he whispered into her ear.

Her arms wrapped tightly around his waist, she nodded. "I can understand that. But you can't..."

"Are you challenging me?" he asked, giving her a devilish grin.

"I give up." She quickly removed plates from the stainless stell stand above the sink before carrying them into the living room where the dining table was.

They all sat down at the table for six, Arun at the head with his wife and Vidyut on both his sides. Just as Vidyut was drawing the chair next to his, Haasini rushed and sat next to Vandana. It was exciting when Vidyut touched her on the sly. But it didn't stop her from feeling nervous. After all, she had met his parents only today. And then there was the pressure that he used to be engaged to her elder sister. She was really keen to make a good impression on them.

Vidyut gave her a mock glare which didn't budge Haasini.

Vandana insisted on serving their guest with her own hands. "Do you like *chicken biryani*?" she asked Haasini.

"It's my favourite, Vandana Aunty. This smells so good," responded Haasini.

"I'll pass on your compliments to the cook," said Vandana with a smile.

Vidyut opened the tall aluminium container which held the fried *papads*, removing a few and placing it on everyone's plate.

"Thanks," said Haasini, taking it from his hand.

"You're welcome, ma'am."

Vandana looked from one to the other. Why was he calling her ma'am? Her husband had mentioned that Haasini was Vidyut's girlfriend. The youngsters of today! Vandana gave a mental shake of her head before passing the bowl of *mosuru bajji* to Vidyut.

Conversation flowed smoothly as they chatted about everything under the weather, Haasini feeling comfortable now that she was out of Vidyut's reach. She ignored the steamy looks he kept throwing in her direction; not really sure how she might react to them.

Vidyut neither touched her nor looked in Haasini's direction when they took the dishes back to the kitchen. A tad hesitant to wake the sleeping tiger, she silently worked along with him, transferring the leftover food into smaller containers before placing everything in the fridge.

Another half an hour later, both Arun and Vandana excused themselves to have their siesta.

Vidyut got up immediately to take Haasini's hand. "Come, let's go to my room."

"I'm not having sex with you, not under your parents' roof, Vidyut." Haasini hesitated at the foot of the stairs, wary of going up with him. "Maybe I'll leave. I…"

He walked down the couple of stairs he had already climbed; lifting her up and throwing her over his left shoulder in a fireman's lift and went up the stairs, taking them two at a time.

Too stunned to say anything, Haasini just hung there on his shoulder until they reached his room.

19

olding her by the waist, Vidyut lifted Haasini off his shoulder to stand her in front of him. He took her face in his hands to kiss her gently, sipping from her lips.

Haasini simply melted, leaning her body into his chest as she gave herself up to his kisses which grew hotter and hotter as the seconds ticked by into minutes. She pulled the hem of his t-shirt out of his jeans to explore his heated skin, her hands tracing the contours of his well-muscled chest.

He, in turn, pulled her t-shirt out of her jeans to caress her waist. "Are you going to refuse me?" he asked, flicking his tongue over the shape of her ear.

She turned her head to better accommodate him, even as she clung to his shoulders for support, her knees feeling like jelly. "You know I can't."

"Then what was that dialogue below stairs?" he enquired, moving away to look down at her blushing face.

She held his face between her hands, speaking to him earnestly, "Please, Vidu. You know I can't resist you. They are your parents and I am sure you feel no awkwardness. But I am meeting them for the first time. What will they think of me if they get to know that I am bedding you even on my first visit to your home?"

Vidyut pushed her away before turning the other way, taking deep breaths to control his libido. It wasn't as if they had not had sex for a long time. They had spent a few hours of every night in the room over his office, making passionate love, the whole of last week. But he only seemed to crave her all the more. She had woven magic around him, his Haasini.

He turned around to place his hands on her slender shoulders. "I'm sorry, babe. I wasn't thinking. Actually, my mind shuts off whenever I am around you. Forgive me?"

Haasini's eyes went wide when she heard his words. She hadn't really been seeking nor expecting an apology. The fact was that she felt adored whenever he touched or kissed her. Placing a hand over his mouth, she shook her head. "Please don't apologise. It thrills me that you want me. I…"

He leaned forward to give her a brief, but hard kiss. "And I can see you want to fuck me whenever I touch you."

She poked her tongue at him, nodding. "That's the truth, yes."

"That makes us even, I suppose." He wrinkled his nose at her.

Brushing her forefinger on his nose, she said, "Thanks for understanding. Shall we go down and sit in the living room?"

"And do what? Hold hands?" he asked, half sarcastically.

"I wouldn't mind," she said, giving him a wink. "Will you?" she asked as an afterthought.

"Hmm… I'd love to," he responded in a hoarse whisper, taking her hand in his before stepping out of the room.

When Vandana went into the living room after her nap, she was pleased to see her son and their guest playing chess. "Let me make coffee."

"I can help you, Aunty."

Vandana waved her back into her chair. "No, my dear, you have done enough work for one day. You continue with your game. I'll get the coffee."

Vidyut grinned mischievously at her, reaching across to trace his thumb over the seam of her lips.

Not to be outdone, Haasini nibbled on the pad of his thumb before rubbing the area with her tongue. "Wanna more?" she asked in a whisper.

He shook his head. "I don't think I can take this love play anymore. My cock is throbbing to get inside you," he growled.

"Hello, Uncle. Did you have a good nap?" Haasini looked beyond Vidyut's shoulder and spoke.

Vidyut quickly brought his hand to his side only to turn his head when she laughed out loud. His father wasn't there in the living room. Realising she had been pulling his leg, he leaned across to take a sharp bite of her lower lip. "You asked for that," he told her.

"I suppose I did. It was yummy." She grinned, having the last word.

At Arun and Vandana's behest, Haasini stayed back for dinner, on the condition—hers—that she prepared *egg burji* and *lachcha parathas*. Both the parents were left licking their fingers clean, praising her cooking skills to the skies. As she cooked, Vidyut quickly whipped a batch of red velvet cupcakes with cream cheese frosting which served as a perfect dessert to end a lovely day.

It was almost eleven when Haasini said her goodbyes. Vidyut left with her in the pretext of dropping her home; the two of them ending up in his room at the café. The foreplay they had indulged in during the afternoon had only made them both all the more eager to make love.

They almost tore off each other's clothes before falling back on the bed. Vidyut nibbled his way from her earlobe to her jawline to the pulse at the crook of her neck while Haasini shivered in his arms even as her hands caressed his velvety back rippling with muscles as hard as steel.

She sighed her pleasure when he stroked the tip of one breast with his damp tongue, thrusting her body closer to him as she held his head, her fingers running through his silky locks. She moaned when he reached out to cup her feminine mound, widening her legs when he thrust a finger into her core. "That feels so good."

"Want me inside?" he asked, his voice hoarse with longing as he thrust two of his fingers rhythmically in and out of her vagina, making her jump off the bed.

"Yes, oh yes!" she moaned, locking her long legs around him when he replaced his fingers with his tumescent manhood. "Vidu…"

"Babe…" He kissed her, plunging his tongue into the warmth of her mouth at the same pace as he thrust his penis into her vagina.

Haasini met him thrust for thrust, rejoicing in the mating ritual which was as old as time, adoring the man in her arms. Sweat beaded on her forehead despite the cold weather as she eagerly awaited the orgasm which promised to catapult her into the stars. No, Haasini didn't believe any longer that orgasm was a myth; not since the first time she had made love with Vidyut. He was a wonderful lover; a giver who always made sure she was totally satisfied before achieving his own peak.

The next hard thrust pushed her over the horizon, making Haasini squeal with delight as the powerful orgasm threw her off her orbit. Clinging to Vidyut, she lifted her hips to meet his rhythmic thrusts before he came soon after; flopping at her side once he was completely spent.

It was a long while before they regained their breaths, grinning at each other. "That was amazing," she said, kissing his rough cheek.

"Truly. You are a fantastic partner in bed, babe." Vidyut rubbed his rough cheek against her soft one.

"So are you. And I've been craving to have you inside me from the moment you touched me in the afternoon," she whispered against his chest.

"When my father was in the office?" he asked, shaking with laughter.

"Yes, you devil. Since then."

"You poor baby. Why didn't you tell me?"

"And what would you have done?"

"Touched you some more."

"Which is exactly why I didn't." She bit his shoulder, leaving her mark.

He pulled her up to close his mouth over a nipple, suckling deeply on it.

"That feels so good, Vidu. Please don't stop."

"Never," he growled before turning his head to her other breast.

It was almost three in the morning when Vidyut dropped her outside her bungalow before taking himself home.

Neither of them noticed the lone figure watching the car as she stood at her bedroom window. Janani stared with a frown on her face as Haasini got out of the front seat of the Audi.

She had gone into Haasini's bedroom to find out if there was something else she could hide which would land her younger sister in trouble; and had been shocked to find that Haasini hadn't been to bed at all. Returning to her own room wondering if she should draw her parents' attention to it, she had been staring out of the window when she saw the car dropping her sister home.

Who was the guy Haasini had been out with? Janani was dying to know. One thing she was convinced about though: that Haasini was the whore she had accused her of being.

Her eyes glinting maliciously, Janani sat back on her bed, planning her revenge. The first step she needed to take was to find out who the man was.

ost in her own world, Haasini didn't notice the burqa clad figure following her to Kamath's Koffee the next day.

Janani had called in sick at the school and standing at the corner bus stop in the pretext of waiting for a bus; her sole purpose being to catch sight of Haasini. When her younger sister stepped out of the compound, Janani pulled the flap of the hired burqa over her face and waited for her to walk ahead before following her a few feet behind.

Janani was surprised when Haasini walked into her ex-fiancé's café. Grimacing, she wondered if she should step in or not. What if Vidyut Kamath saw her at his café? She didn't want him to think that Janani was chasing him; not after breaking off their engagement.

Just then, Janani remembered she was covered from head to feet and no one could find out her identity. With a smile of triumph, she walked into the coffee shop and looked to her right and then to her left before spotting Haasini at a corner table.

So! Haasini was here to work. Janani quickly went to the counter to place an order for a cold coffee, paying for it in cash. She walked left and sat at a table not far from

Haasini, sipping on her coffee once it was delivered. It wasn't too bad! And the amount they charged for it—no less than two hundred rupees—was equal to daylight robbery. Was this the business Vidyut was so enamoured with that he had quit his high-end job? Wasn't it a good thing she had dumped him? Or she would soon have been tying the knot with a foolish businessman.

Janani grinned maliciously to herself, feeling good that no one would be able to see it. She frowned when she saw Haasini typing furiously away into her laptop. What did she do all day? Did it make any kind of money or was it all time pass? Just now, Janani wouldn't have minded being a fly on the wall right behind Haasini. She knew for a fact that her younger sister was an idiot. How could she not be? After all, she had run away with a good-for-nothing fellow. And she hadn't denied it when Janani had accused her of sleeping with the man.

Janani gnashed her teeth. Some people could easily get away with murder. And Haasini was definitely one of those.

Soon, she was bored sitting there waiting for something to happen. Only, nothing did. A waiter delivered coffee and some snacks at Haasini's table. Her sister continued to work, stopping now and again to munch on the food or drink from her tall glass.

Tch! *Why the hell didn't I carry my earphones?* That way, Janani could have entertained herself watching videos on YouTube. How many times to check her updates on Facebook, Twitter, and Instagram? It wasn't even as if she was all that active on social media.

She scrolled down the Facebook page, curious to find out if Haasini had an account. When she searched for Haasini Rai, the first name which came up was her sister's. With a feral growl, Janani checked the page which was full of pictures and links. So! Haasini wrote for several newspapers, for their entertainment sections. She reviewed movies and what was this? A discotheque? Ugh! What was a family girl like Haasini doing at a disco? *Che che!* Wasn't it a good thing not too many people other than those in their close neighbourhood knew of their relationship? Janani was too ashamed to call Haasini her sister.

She scrolled some more and found a link to the article in Bombay Express. It was a review about Kamath's Koffee. Opening the link, Janani noticed that it was a 5-star review. Was the coffee shop that good? She quickly read the piece, unable to ignore the fact that it was very well covered, mentioning every aspect of the café—the ambience, the staff, the service, the food, and the costing. Huh! So, what was the big deal? Anyone could write such an article.

Just as Janani shut the link, she noticed a tall figure walking out from behind the counter. It was Vidyut. He looked dashing in a pair of cotton slacks and t-shirt and an apron which carried the café's logo of KK entwined together in a stylish font. The burqa gave her all the privacy she required so that she could check him out thoroughly. Despite being engaged to the man for six months, Janani had never had the confidence to look him in the eye or check out his looks. Just now, she almost drooled at his lean and sleekly muscled body when he strode across the coffee shop. For a moment, she thought he had noticed her and almost had a heart attack before she saw him walk further, towards the corner table where Haasini was sitting.

Jealousy burnt like acid in her throat when Janani saw him sit down across from Haasini. And what did the whore do? She simply shut down her laptop to grin at him, chatting with him nineteen to a dozen. Agreed, she had reviewed his coffee shop. But that still didn't warrant such a degree of familiarity. But then, Janani knew her sister was a flirt. Haasini probably chased men for all Janani knew. She glared in their direction as Vidyut sat there for a while, his laughter ringing out again and again.

Damn! What the hell was so funny?! She didn't have a great opinion about Haasini's sense of humour. And what was with the man? He had spoken barely a sentence or two the few times they had been out together. Janani conveniently forgot that it took two people to hold a dialogue and she had never bothered to respond to Vidyut except in monosyllables.

Just now, watching them chat, Janani writhed with jealousy. She sat there, glaring at them, wondering when he would get up and go away. Didn't he have work to do? After all, he was the owner of the coffee shop. And she couldn't help noticing that business was booming. All the tables were full. Someone had even claimed the chair across from hers and shifted it to another table.

She surreptitiously checked her watch. It was past noon. She had been sitting here for two hours and Vidyut had been chatting with Haasini for at least one-fourth of the time. What the hell was going on?

A sudden spark hit Janani. Was he the man who had dropped Haasini home last night? They had come in an Audi. Both her eyes and mouth went wide in shock. Oh yes! Her fiancé used to drive an Audi.

What the hell!

Was Haasini flirting, probably sleeping with the man who used to be engaged to Janani?

Janani jumped up from her chair and abruptly walked out of the café, uncaring that she almost pushed aside a customer who was stepping in; her mind in a turmoil.

How could this be? Like a typical dog in the manger, Janani didn't want Haasini to have what could not be hers. She was ready to go to any lengths to break the relationship between Vidyut and Haasini.

Pulling the burqa off, she shoved it into the large bag she was carrying, walking furiously down the road, and reaching her bungalow. Shoving open the gate, she walked into the compound and then on into her house; completely on auto-pilot. She forgot that she was supposed to be working at school.

"Janani? How come you are home so early?" Jyothi called out from the sofa where she was sitting, working on some embroidery. When her daughter didn't reply, she asked, "Is everything alright?"

Janani was furious, her face red in consequence. "Do you know where your daughter goes every day?" she snarled at her mother.

"Are you talking about Haasini?" asked Jyothi in a calm voice. She was very well aware that her younger born was working from a coffee shop.

"Who else? So? Do you know?"

Jyothi gave her a nod before continuing with her handwork.

"Mom!" Janani screamed, walking across the living room to sit next to her mother. She had a good mind to shake the older woman until her teeth rattled.

What kind of a woman was she to allow her daughter to behave however she wanted? Didn't she feel any shame that Haasini flirted with strange men? It was worse this time round. She was flirting—probably having an affair—with her own sister's ex-fiancé. How horrible was that?! "Are you aware that Haasini goes to a coffee shop to work?"

Jyothi looked up from her embroidery, a small scowl on her face. "What are you talking about? That Haasini works at a coffee shop? Then how can she also write on her laptop? Are you sure about it, Janani?" she asked.

Janani stamped her foot in frustration. "Mom! I am not saying she's working for the coffee shop. She goes there, day after day, to do her work."

The scowl cleared from Jyothi's forehead. "*Haan, haan.* That's what I thought." She bent down to focus on what she was doing much to her elder daughter's annoyance.

"Don't you mind?"

"Why should I mind?" This time, Jyothi didn't even lift her head to look at Janani, giving her full concentration to the task at hand.

"But Mom! She's flirting with every man who crosses her path." Janani got up to stand in front of her mother, her stance threatening as she did her best to get her point across.

This time, the frown was way heavier on Jyothi's forehead. "Don't be silly, Janani. Haasini would never do that."

"Really?" Janani's eyebrows rose up, almost touching her hairline. "Isn't that why she ran away with Yeshwant?" Her tone was highly sarcastic.

Jyothi sighed. "That's water under the bridge, the incident more than two years old. Why don't you just forget it? Haasini came to her senses within three months and is way more sensible nowadays."

"Huh! You are being stupid, Mom, to believe everything she tells you. Haasini hasn't changed, not at all."

Jyothi gave up on her embroidery, placing the cloth, needle, and skeins of embroidery thread on a side table to give Janani her complete attention. "I think you aren't being fair, Janani. Do cut her some slack! She's working so hard and has made a success of herself. Do you know that four big newspaper dailies publish her reviews regularly?" The mother couldn't stop feeling proud of her younger daughter.

Acrimonious jealousy burned like acid within Janani's innards. Here she was trying to call her mother's attention to Haasini's irresponsible behaviour and all her mother had to offer was to sing the damn girl's praises. Grr!

"What does that matter when people are laughing at her reputation? Haasini is a flirt! She spends all her time with men; not really caring who they are."

Jyothi got up from the sofa, obviously agitated. Her husband had been right. Janani disliked her younger sister, totally. Not at all keen on taking sides—after all, they both were her own flesh and blood—Jyothi tried to pacify her eldest born. "Listen, Janani. I am sure you are mistaken. If nothing, Haasini won't have the time. How can she when she's working so hard, day and night?" What the mother didn't let on to Janani was that Haasini had made a lot of money in the past few years. She didn't want to fan Janani's jealousy even more.

"Working hard, my foot! You didn't see what I saw today, Mom."

"And what did you see?" asked Jyothi, fast losing her patience.

"Haasini was sitting in Kamath's Koffee, flirting with Vidyut Kamath." Janani went to sit back on the sofa, glad now that she had finally dropped the bomb over her mother's head.

A thoroughly miffed Jyothi said, "So what? Why do you care? After all, you threw the ring in his face. Why are you bothered if your sister likes the man?" She was simply being flippant, not really believing there was anything serious between Haasini and Vidyut. Jyothi was still pissed off with Janani about the broken engagement.

"Mom? What's wrong with you, Mom? How can you support Haasini so blindly? And you are blaming me for the broken engagement. What about dad? He was the one who objected to Vidyut's sudden change of career. He only asked me to go and talk to him about it. He…"

Jyothi raised a hand and stopped Janani in mid-sentence. "Enough! I don't want to hear any more about the matter. We have been through this only too many times. And what is the use? There's no way it's possible to set right a relationship which has been broken. Now tell me, I'm going to make tea. Do you want some?"

Janani wanted to throw something; even bang her head on the wall. Such was her anger and frustration.

Realising that whatever she said now would fall on deaf ears, she simply gave a nod. "I'll also have tea."

Once her mother went inside the kitchen, Janani paced the living room. It looked like her mother wasn't ready to deal with Haasini. And she was sure her father—especially in the mood he was in after the laptop incident—would not speak against Haasini. It was left to Janani to deal with the situation.

And deal with it I will! She swore to herself.

21

Vandana waited to talk to her son at the first opportunity. On Tuesday, during dinner, she asked Vidyut, "Do you like Haasini?"

Vidyut looked up from his plate of *neer dosa* teamed with *chicken curry*. "Yes, *Amma,* I like her."

"Vidu likes her enough to marry her," declared Arun, not to be left out of the conversation. He behaved as if Haasini was his very own discovery.

"Hmm… if she agrees, yes." Vidyut was yet to speak to her about marriage. He was a tad hesitant mainly because she was Janani's sister. Vidyut had a good mind to simply elope with Haasini. But somehow, he didn't think she would be ready to commit the same mistake twice in her life; bringing down the wrath of her parents on her head.

"Why wouldn't she agree to marry you?" asked Vandana. The mother felt that her son was too good for any woman on earth.

Vidyut sighed. "Haasini is Janani's younger sister."

Vandana's mouth fell open in surprise as she looked from one man to the other. "Are you talking about the same Janani you were engaged to?" she asked in a shocked voice.

Vidyut nodded, without saying anything.

"But how? Haresh and Jyothi never mentioned they had another child. I always thought they had only one daughter." She turned to ask her husband, "When did you get to know about their second child?"

Arun nodded, saying, "I also thought the same until yesterday. I…"

"And when were you going to tell me about it?" asked Vandana, thoroughly miffed with her husband.

"Listen, Vandana. There's no need to be angry. I met Haasini only yesterday, same as you. But when we were talking, I asked her about her family and realised she was Janani's sister. I…"

"How can you be so foolish, Vidu?" Vandana left her husband alone to turn around and attack her son. "Can't you find someone else for a girlfriend?"

"Why, *Amma*? Don't you like Haasini?" asked Vidyut, only half serious.

"That's not the point, is it?" Vandana glared at him as if it was all his mistake that Haasini was Janani's sister. "There must be hundreds of eligible girls in Bengaluru. Of all of them, you had to choose your ex-fiancée's sister. What do you see in Haasini that you did not see in Janani?"

Vidyut considered his mother's question for a few moments before answering her patiently. "I see a world of difference, *Amma*. They couldn't be more unlike each other."

"I agree with Vidu; even though I don't know Janani all that well. That girl never spoke more than a word or two at one time. And look how sweet Haasini is. She's very intelligent too." Arun was all praise for Haasini.

"I agree with all that," said Vandana. "I also like Haasini a lot. While I didn't really know Janani well enough to like or dislike her. But how will their parents agree to this match?" She was genuinely worried.

Vidyut was a tad bothered about it as well. Not that he was very particular whether Haasini's parents gave their consent. Only he knew that Haasini will not agree to marry him unless she had her parents' blessings.

"Let me speak to Haresh Rai," offered Arun. However strict a father he was, his children's happiness counted a lot with him. And Vidyut was the apple of his eye.

"Wait for a couple of weeks, *Appa*. Let me convince Haasini first. Please?" Vidyut placed a hand on his father's shoulder to persuade him.

Arun gave a slow nod. "If that's what you want."

"Yes, *Appa*." Vidyut got up from the dining table, quickly clearing it before wiping it clean. "If you guys will excuse me? I need to meet a friend."

While both parents guessed who the friend was, they didn't say anything, waving to him as he left.

A couple of hours later, Vidyut held Haasini close to his chest as he sat leaning against the bedhead. "I love you, babe." He brushed his lips over the pulse at her neck even as he cupped his hands over her luscious breasts.

Tilting her head on his shoulder, her hands on his arms, Haasini gave a soft sigh, totally satiated by their lovemaking barely a few minutes ago. "Mmm… I love you too, Vidu."

"Marry me?" he asked, turning her around to face him, his hand at her chin.

She turned her slumberous gaze up to his. "I'd love to, sweetheart. But how do we go about it?"

"My father says he will speak with yours."

"Arun Uncle would do that?" she asked, her eyes shining with happiness.

"Yes. My parents like you a lot. And let me tell you upfront. Neither of them really cared for Janani. Not that any of us knew her well enough to like or dislike her." Vidyut grimaced.

"I don't know what to say." Haasini buried her face in his shoulder, hugging him close.

"Let me ask *Appa* to speak to Haresh Uncle this weekend then."

She nodded. "Thank you," she whispered, kissing him on his cheek.

"Don't be so damn formal," he growled, nuzzling her cheek before kissing her mouth. They made long and leisurely love once again before he took her home.

Janani, who had been waiting at her window, watching out for Haasini's return home, decided she should do something about it that very day. She simply couldn't stomach the fact that her sister was happy while she, Janani, wasn't.

When Haasini left home with her laptop in the morning, Janani followed her once again, wearing the burqa. She had a vague plan in place. Anything to create trouble in paradise!

Janani settled down in the middle of the coffee shop, her eyes trained on the counter. Anytime now, Vidyut would come out to greet Haasini who was seated in the furthest corner like the last time.

She wasn't mistaken. Soon, Vidyut stepped out from behind the counter and walked over to Haasini, sitting in the chair opposite hers and chatting with her as if there was no tomorrow. Janani's jaw ached with the way she gritted her teeth, too angry for words. How dare Haasini flirt with the guy Janani was supposed to have married? That the engagement was well and truly broken, that too at Janani's instigation, didn't seem to count.

It was a long time, almost twenty minutes, before Vidyut got up. Janani didn't miss the flying kiss he blew in her sister's direction, her blood pressure rising more than ever. She eyed him walking back to the counter and further into the kitchen.

Janani got up and walked right behind him, asking the girl at the counter where the washroom was. When she pointed her to a door next to the kitchen, Janani went there. She came across a small corridor which had three doors. Two led to the men's and women's cloak rooms and the third one was further down, at the end. Curious, she walked over to check the door. It was open. She went in and realised it was an office with a large desk in the middle, a swivelling chair at the back and two visitors' chairs. There was a filing cabinet at the back. Everything appeared fairly new. This must definitely be Vidyut's office, concluded Janani.

Should I wait for him to turn up? And what should I do when he did? Before Janani could come up with a plan, the man himself stepped in, speaking to someone over his shoulder.

"Can you manage to get the stock, Nirmal? I don't know why they have delayed until the last minute. I…"

"No worries, sir. I'll go right now. I've already called Vivek. He should be here in ten minutes and takeover the rest of my shift." Vivek was another student who was in Vidyut's employ.

"That's awesome, buddy. Thanks a ton," said Vidyut, slapping the younger man on his shoulder. Walking to his table, he sat down to open a drawer with a key. That was when he noticed the burqa clad figure.

"Who's this?" asked Vidyut, surprised.

Janani pulled the burqa off to reveal her identity.

"You!" Vidyut couldn't believe his eyes. What the hell was his ex-fiancée doing here in his office, of all places? And she had sneaked in, obviously. Otherwise, why wear a burqa? He usually kept his office locked. But he had left it barely a couple of minutes ago to get something from the kitchen. And she had obviously sneaked in during that gap.

"Hello, Vidyut!" Janani spoke in a hoarse voice, her throat all dried up. Was it her imagination or had he grown handsomer in the past few months? And his body language screamed "success". Had she made a mistake in letting him go? She frowned. It was all her father's fault. He had only brainwashed her into believing that Vidyut wouldn't make her a good husband, not if he ran his own business.

"What are you doing here?" asked Vidyut. He shut his eyes and prayed for patience before lifting a hand. "Wait! I need to finish something urgent here." Removing a bill for the goods which hadn't been delivered, he handed it to Nirmal and said, "Here you go. Thanks, pal."

"Not at all, sir. Er… do you need me to…?" Nirmal gave Vidyut's unexpected guest a corner-eyed glance.

Vidyut gave a small shake of his head. "I'll see you soon, Nirmal."

"To what do I owe this visit, Janani?" asked Vidyut. He wouldn't have thought twice before throwing her out of his office, except for the fact that she was the older sister of the woman he loved; the one he wished to marry.

"Er… Vidyut, I came to apologise." Janani lied through her teeth. Walking forward, she asked, "May I sit down?"

Vidyut's instincts screamed even as he grimaced. He wasn't at all keen for Janani to sit down in his office. Nor did he want to have a cosy chat with her. Pointing a hand to one of the chairs across his desk, he tilted his head.

Janani settled down and looked at him. "Won't you offer me a cup of coffee? For old times' sake?" she asked in a throaty voice.

Feeling cornered, Vidyut lifted the intercom and asked for two espressos, his voice guttural with tension. He didn't like the present situation, not one little bit. Just then, he remembered something. "Why were you wearing a burqa?" he asked, frowning at Janani.

She laughed, the sound grating on his ears. "Just like that. You know how people are. They tend to gossip. I didn't want anyone to know I was coming here to meet you."

Strange! She had never shown interest in meeting him, openly or secretly, during the months they were engaged. Why now?

"Is that why you came? To meet me?" he asked, pinning her with his burning golden gaze.

"Yes! Listen, Vidyut. I think I made a mistake. I…"

He raised a hand to stop her from speaking further. "I don't want to know. Please have the coffee and leave."

Janani, being stubborn as a mule, spoke to him—a lot—astounding Vidyut. He had never heard her utter more than a monosyllable. She told him how sorry she was that she had returned his ring to him; about how pleased she was about his success with his business; how her father was the one to blame for their broken engagement; so on and so forth.

In the meanwhile, Seema was desperate as she placed two mugs of espressos on a tray, adding four packets of sugar and tissues to it. She was already filling up the next tray, her mind in a turmoil. They were short of hands as Nirmal had left to follow Vidyut's instructions and Vivek was yet to arrive. How was she going to get this tray to Vidyut's office?

Haasini walked to the counter right on cue. "Hey Seema. You look frazzled. Need help?"

"Er… ma'am." She nodded before shaking her head. She wasn't sure it would be right, asking a guest to make the delivery.

"Come on, Seema. Tell me. I see Nirmal isn't around."

"Yes, ma'am. He had to leave urgently to get some much-needed stock. His replacement hasn't arrived yet. Everyone else is busy. I…"

Haasini took the tray which was on the counter. "So, tell me. Where do I deliver this?"

"Ma'am… are you sure?"

"Yes," said Haasini firmly.

"It's for Vidyut sir, in his office."

"Okay. I'll take care of it." Haasini walked further behind the counter.

"Thank you, ma'am," called out a relieved Seema.

Haasini waved a hand in her direction before walking towards Vidyut's cabin, a bright smile on her face. Two cups of coffee! Had he ordered one for her as well? She expected him to call or ping her any second now. With a swing to her slender hips, she went to the door and pushed it open, saying, "Tat-ta-da…"

The tray fell out of Haasini's hand, the mugs shattering, the hot coffee splashing all over the place. Her eyes almost fell out of her head as she stared at the scene in front of her—Janani comfortably ensconced in Vidyut's lap, her arms wrapped around his neck.

Haasini turned and fled from the scene, not bothering to respond to Vidyut who called out to her, shouting her name again and again.

V idyut completely lost his cool, throwing a couple of plates across his pristine kitchen, watching with dubious satisfaction as they smashed to smithereens. That there was no one to witness the bull's temper tantrum was a good thing, as it wasn't a pretty sight.

Women!

Just now, he didn't want to have anything to do with them. Complete idiots! No! They were absolute schemers! No no! He shook his head vigorously. Women were expert manipulators! That's what they were. And their minds were all twisted. Nothing like a man's mind which could only relate to simple logic.

Today, he had got the shock of his life when Janani visited him, not realising that the worst was yet to come.

They had been talking for one minute, Janani telling him that she was ready to get back with him. Just when he was explaining to her that it was simply not possible, she suddenly landed in his lap, her arms strangling his neck. Before he could push her away, Haasini had walked in.

Okay! Agreed that the situation had been sticky. But why the hell couldn't Haasini wait for him to explain what was going on? How could she simply run away from the scene? Where was her common sense? If he had told her once, he had told her a hundred times that he loved her. Couldn't she trust him not to two-time her; that too with her own sister?

And as for Janani,,, the woman had never spoken one full sentence with him. What had come over the woman? And there had never been anything physical between the two. They hadn't even held hands. The only time he had taken her hand in his had been when he had placed his ring on her finger, in the midst of their families and two-hundred-odd guests.

What the hell had come over her that she had jumped into his lap?

If he had called Haasini once, he had called her a dozen times. In the beginning, the phone just rang and rang. But soon after, it had been switched off!

Was it a wonder he was feeling murderous by now?

Women! Vidyut punched his fist into a granite counter and swore virulently when he almost broke his fingers.

Janani sat on her bed, an evil grin splitting her face in two as she gazed into her phone. Her mind wasn't on the messages, but on the scene at Vidyut's office. She laughed out loud when she recalled the appalled expression on her sister's face. It was a sheer stroke of luck that Janani had heard footsteps outside the office. Quickly thinking on her feet, she had jumped into Vidyut's lap. After all, whoever was outside, would be a witness to their "supposed" lovemaking.

But she had been beyond thrilled when she saw that it was Haasini at the door. Hahaha! Her younger sister's expression had been priceless even as the tray fell out of her hands. And the foolish girl, she hadn't waited to listen to Vidyut's explanation and had simply run away. Serve them both right! How dare they get together behind Janani's back?

All the people her family knew—their friends, relatives, and neighbours—would laugh their heads off if they got to know that Vidyut had rejected the elder sister and got together with the younger one. No, it didn't matter that it was Janani who had rejected him. No one would bother to take that point into consideration.

As for Vidyut, he couldn't have been ruder. He had pushed Janani out of his lap, not bothering to look back when she fell on the floor, hurting her hip in the process. He had rushed after Haasini, uncaring about the mess she had left behind in his office, spilt coffee, and smashed china all over the place. While it hadn't been difficult for Vidyut to step on the broken crockery with his shoe-clad feet as he left the office, Janani had had such a difficult time walking out in her flat slippers. Huh!

Stepping into the café, Janani had been thoroughly chuffed when she noted that Haasini was nowhere in sight while Vidyut appeared like a madman as he tried to reach her repeatedly on her cell phone.

Janani cackled with laughter. Good! They deserved to be unhappy. And she was glad she had managed to bring it about.

"Haasini…" Haresh touched his daughter's bowed head. She looked as if the whole world had shattered around her. "What is wrong, my child?"

Haasini shook her head, refusing to look up at her father. What could she tell him? That she was in love with her own sister's ex-fiancé who maybe wasn't an ex after all?

Janani hated her. She had accepted that. So, she didn't find anything strange in her behaviour. But Vidyut? He had obviously ordered two coffees for himself and Janani. And they had appeared so cosy as he held her in his arms. How many times had Haasini sat in his lap in the same office chair in the past week?

She rubbed her face with both her hands, trying to stop the tears which refused to be checked. *I loved him! I trusted him! How could he do this to me?*

"Talk to me, Haasini," said her father in a soft voice even as he ran his hand gently over the top of her head.

"You wouldn't understand, Dad," she said in a choked voice. "My life is all over."

Haresh bit his lip to stop himself from laughing. He was only too aware of the Cancer crab's tendency to be melodramatic. He could see that something was wrong. But he couldn't believe there was no solution to the issue. "Why don't you try me?"

She shook her head vigorously. "No, Dad. At least, not now. I'm too disturbed. Maybe we can talk tomorrow?"

"If that's what you want." He reached into his pocket when his phone vibrated against his hip. It was almost eleven. Who could be calling him at this hour? His eyes went wide when he saw Vidyut Kamath's name. Getting up quickly, he walked to the balcony to speak in private, not keen to disturb his already troubled daughter.

"Hello, Haresh Uncle. I know it's late and I'm sorry to trouble you. But the matter is urgent."

"Hello, Vidyut. Not at all. We can talk."

"I'm outside your house. Could you please come out?"

"Oh! Why don't you come in, my boy? I know what Janani did to you wasn't right. And I apologise for it. I…"

Vidyut shook his head before realising that Haasini's father wouldn't be able to see him. "No, no, Uncle. That's all fine. But could you please come out?"

A small frown on his forehead, Haresh turned to look at his younger daughter slouched on the sofa. She didn't really need him, at least not immediately. And he knew for a fact that Haasini was strong. He quickly thrust the house keys into his pocket and his feet into a pair rubber chappals and walked out of his bungalow, shutting the door quietly behind him.

Vidyut got out of his car to greet Haresh with a handshake.

"What's up, Vidyut? I hope everything is well," said Haresh, seeing the unhappy expression on the younger man's face. He still couldn't make peace with the fact that Janani had let go of such a nice man. Vidyut would have made her an amazing husband, and more than that, he would have made Haresh and Jyothi a wonderful son-in-law.

"Not really, Uncle. I need your help." He opened the door to the passenger seat. "If you are okay with it, we can go to my coffee shop which is not all that far away."

Haresh looked at the younger man curiously. What must be so urgent and important that Vidyut had sought him out so late at night? "Sure, Vidyut. I don't mind."

Vidyut quickly drove over to the café, opening the side door to let them inside. Once they were seated at a table with two mugs of freshly brewed filter coffee, he spoke, "Uncle, I'm sorry about the mess I am in right now. And more than that, I am sorry to drag you into it." Taking a deep breath, he burst out, "I'm in love with Haasini. I…"

"Wait a minute!" Haresh raised his hand to stop Vidyut in mid-sentence, "Are you talking about my *younger* daughter, Haasini?"

Vidyut nodded vigorously before giving a long monologue while Haresh listened, not interrupting the younger man. He explained how he and Haasini had met and become close before either of them realised the connection with Janani. "I'm sorry, Uncle. I mean no offence to Janani, but there was nothing between us, no spark, no interest, no chemistry. But Haasini is everything to me, Uncle; she's my whole life. I love her from the bottom of my heart."

"What about Haasini? Does she return your feelings?" Haresh couldn't help smiling. After all, it looked like God had answered his prayers. He had wished that Vidyut should become his son-in-law and see what had happened.

"Yes, Uncle, she does," said Vidyut, colour running up his lean cheeks when it struck him powerfully that he was speaking with the father of the woman he loved.

Haresh's smile turned broader. "You both have my blessings, my boy. Just the one thing: I hope you'll agree to a long engagement; not too long, only till the time I find a groom for my elder daughter. I am sure you understand that I can't get my younger child married while the elder one is still unmarried. I…"

Vidyut took Haresh's hand in both of his. "Thank you so much, Uncle. You truly have a big heart. Actually, *Appa* was going to call you next week. But…"

"No, no. As the girl's father, it's my duty to get in touch with your parents. I'll call him tomorrow itself. I…"

Vidyut shook his head, a broken expression on his face.

That's when Haresh recalled a similar expression on Haasini's face. If they both loved each other, what was the problem? Haresh asked Vidyut outright.

Hesitantly, with a lot of hemming and hawing, Vidyut narrated to his would-be father-in-law all that had happened at the café today.

Haresh's face grew darker and darker as Vidyut spoke about Janani's behaviour and how Haasini refused to even talk to him after that. "I can convince Haasini of the truth if only she will let me. But she's refusing to even take my call. I'm totally lost, Uncle. She's so young and impulsive, with a tendency to rush headlong where angels fear to tread, if you know what I mean," he appealed to Haresh, who nodded in agreement.

"Just now, she doesn't trust me. I…" Vidyut jumped off his chair to walk up and down, his temper getting the better of him. Returning to the table after pacing for a few minutes, he sat in front of Haresh to say, "Uncle, I don't know how to deal with the situation. If Janani was some stranger, I would have dealt with her differently. But she happens to be the sister of the woman I love; I want to marry. How can I insult her? You have to help me, Uncle. I…"

It was Haresh's turn to take Vidyut's hand in both of his. "Leave it all to me, son. I am blessed to have you for my son-in-law. And thank you for forgiving me and my family. You don't know how happy I am that Haasini has someone like you to care for her."

A glimmer of a smile finally appeared on Vidyut's face, the first time he smiled at Haresh that evening. "Thank you, Uncle."

Haresh got up. "Let's go home. Haasini is there and you can speak to her."

Which is what Vidyut had hoped for. His smile broader and lighter, he got up to walk to the door with Haasini's father.

Neither man was aware of the shock which awaited them at the Rais' residence. Haasini had disappeared, without leaving a note unlike the last time she had run away.

23

aasini checked into a hotel for the night. She felt she couldn't live under the same roof as her sister who had got back together with the man Haasini loved.

When she realised that her father had gone out of the house, she quickly got up to pack an overnight case and took it with her along with the backpack containing her laptop. She hailed an auto-rickshaw and requested the driver to drop her at Radisson Bengaluru City Center in Ulsoor. She booked herself a room through the Makemytrip website on the way.

Checking in, Haasini sat in the middle of the bed and cried her heart out. She had to find an accommodation soon, at least until Janani married Vidyut and left for her husband's home. Maybe after that, Haasini could go back to live with her parents.

She cried some more before sudden anger put a stop to her tears. How dare Vidyut two-time her and her sister? How dare he?

Haasini slapped her forehead in frustration. Why the hell did she have to fall in love with her sister's ex-fiancé of all people?

Yes, he was tall and handsome; and there was the fact that he was so successful at his business. She sat up straight. Is that why Janani was ready to take him back? After all, her father and Janani hadn't liked the idea of Vidyut setting up a start-up instead of the lucrative job he had held. Now that Janani had seen how successful his coffee shop was, it looked like she was keen to marry him.

But what about Vidyut? Hadn't he professed to love her—Haasini? Jealousy burned like acid through her veins as she recalled the last time when she had seen him; with Janani sitting comfortably in his lap, her arms locked around his neck. The picture played in her mind repeatedly, whether she had her eyes open or shut.

And had he been protesting? Not at all!

Haasini jumped up from the bed to walk to the window and stare out of it, rubbing a hand over her burning eyes. Had he always liked Janani more? But hadn't said anything because Janani had refused to marry him?

That must be it! But now that Janani was ready to take him back, Vidyut had gone back to his fiancée. Yes, Janani wasn't his ex any longer. They were back together; for good this time.

And I had better accept it! Haasini told herself firmly. When the area at the centre of the bed lit up, she turned her gaze to her blinking phone which was on silent. Seeing her father's face on the screen, she took the call.

"Dad! I'm sorry, Dad. I shouldn't have left home without leaving a note. I would have eventually left a message on your phone; after I felt a little better. I…"

"Haasini…" Her father's voice was hoarse, both worry and temper vying with each other as he gritted his teeth to gain his lost patience. "Where are you?"

Haasini shook her head. "Does it matter, Dad? Suffice to say I am safe."

"You never did tell me what you were upset about. Talk to me, Haasini." He spoke in a compulsive voice, willing her to confide in him.

"Dad…" Haasini wailed, tears flowing down her cheeks. "What to say, Dad? My luck for having the perfect life partner seems non-existent. First, I fell for the useless Yeshwant. Now, I have fallen for a man who can never be mine." She howled uncontrollably.

"What? What are you talking about? Why can't the man you love become yours?" asked Haresh. He rolled his eyes as he turned to look at Vidyut. Neither man noticed Janani standing at the entrance to her room, watching the two of them.

"Dad! You don't know the half of it, Dad. Vidyut loves Janani. Please get them married as soon as possible. I…"

"You're an idiot, babe. No, not babe. You are a baby. I was right all along. You are too damn young. It was my fault I fell in love with someone such as you. Goodbye, Haasini." Vidyut cut the call. He had taken the phone from Haresh when the latter offered it to him. But hearing Haasini say that her father should get Vidyut and Janani married had come as a rude shock. He was beyond furious now.

Haasini stared at her silent phone. She had been speaking to her father. How did Vidyut come online right in the middle of the conversation? And how dare he accuse her of being too young for him? *I'll show him!*

She called him on speed-dial.

Not having to think twice, Vidyut took her call. "What now?" he growled.

"How dare you say I'm too young for you? How dare you? If you wanted to go back to Janani, why didn't you just tell me so to my face? Don't you have the guts to face up to the truth? It was so damn mean of you, Vidu, to let me find out the way I did. I…"

"Are you done?" he snarled.

"Huh?"

"I asked you if you're done with the crap you're spouting."

"You… you… I want to murder you. How dare you trample on my feelings? You really have no idea how much you have hurt me, do you? You…?"

"Where the hell are you hiding? Do you have the guts to tell me? Do you have the audacity to spout all your abuses to my face? Do you, Haasini?"

Janani felt goosebumps all over her person when she heard Vidyut speak to Haasini on the phone. She could sense his love and passion for her sister and felt tears in her own eyes. Had she made a terrible mistake? She quickly did an about turn and shut herself in her room, sitting down to think.

In the meanwhile, Haasini said, "Come over if you're courageous enough to face an a furious lioness. I'm at Radisson Bengaluru City Center, Ulsoor. In room no…" Hearing the dial tone with disgust, Haasini threw her phone on the bed, hugging herself tightly as she walked up and down the room.

What was Vidyut going to do? What excuse could he have for holding Janani in his lap, her arms around his neck? Haasini fumed, her temper refusing to cool down.

Hearing a knock on her door, Haasini peeped through the keyhole. Surprised to see Vidyut outside—after all, it had been barely fifteen minutes since she told him where she was; and how had the hotel management let him come up to her room?

"Open the door, Haasini! Or I might have to knock it down."

"You wouldn't!" Haasini opened the door to glare at him.

Vidyut pushed his way into the room before turning to glare right back at her. "You should have let me try. Believe me, I would have knocked the door down."

"The hotel people would have had you arrested."

"You have high hopes."

A curious frown on her face, she asked, "How did they let you get this far?"

He tilted his chin at her, giving her a snooty glance. "I have friends in high places." One of the hotel partners had been in school with Vidyut from Std I to X. Not that he planned to tell her about it, at least not now.

"Oh! I should have known. So, what are you doing here?"

"You were giving me some advice over the phone. Why don't you say it to my face?"

"Regarding what?" she asked, pretending not to understand; her whole body thrumming with excitement despite the temper which rode high in them both. In spite of the fact that he was furious, his anger coming forth in fumes, he looked too bloody handsome; hot actually. All she wanted to do was to throw herself into his arms.

But no! He didn't belong to her; but to her sister Janani.

Her face growing dark with sorrow, Haasini said, "Why are you here? You obviously love Janani. Which is why I got out of the picture: so that I don't embarrass either of you with my presence. Just go away and marry her. Go!" She turned the other way, her arms protectively folded across her chest as it heaved with misery.

"I have a good mind to put you across my knees and give you the spanking of your life."

She turned around in a flash, her eyes sparkling with temper. "YOU WOULDN'T DARE!"

He swiftly lifted her up in his arms and plonked down on the only chair, pushing her face down over his lap.

When she screamed 'no', he slapped her on her bottom, his temper getting completely out of hand.

"Viduuuuuuuuuuu…"

"Do you wanna more?"

She turned her head, her hair tumbling all over her face as she glared at him. "Have you gone mad?"

"Yes, stark, raving, mad." He pushed her off his lap down to the carpet and jumped off the chair. "What else will a man become when he falls in love with a child like you?" The Taurus bull mooed louder than ever, almost shaking the walls of the room.

Her mouth fell open as Haasini stared at him, more fascinated than horrified by his temper. The truth was that he thrilled her beyond measure. She decided to ignore him calling her a child. After all, it seemed as if she had behaved like one.

Does he truly love me? Was I mistaken? It was only when Vidyut roared again did Haasini realise she had spoken the words aloud.

"Of course, I do, you she-cat. And yes, you are totally mistaken. Your bitch of a sister threw herself into my arms the moment she heard someone outside the door—which was you. Barely half a minute earlier, she was sitting on the chair across my table. And did you allow me to explain? No!" He mooed all the louder. "You just ran away. I am not sure I can live the whole of my life with a woman who runs away from situations every time something happens."

Thinking back, Haasini could see that she had been mighty foolish imagining Vidyut had got back with her sister. She walked forward to stand close to him, chest to chest. "Can you live with this woman if she promises not to run away, not under any circumstance?" she asked, speaking in a whisper.

"Never ever?" he asked, his voice a softer growl at her close proximity. "I want you to swear on your life."

"I swear to never, ever, run away from situations," she said, peeping up at him through her drenched eyelashes before reaching forward to place a hand on the top of his head in a promise.

Vidyut had a difficult time not laughing at her puppy dog expression. Biting his lip, he asked, "What if you do?"

"You can put me on your knees and spank me all you want," she offered.

"That doesn't seem like a fit enough punishment," he protested. "Did you by any chance enjoy the spanking?" His voice shook with laughter.

Haasini burst out laughing, nodding vigorously. "A little too much."

"You are going to be the death of me, woman." He grabbed her close to his chest, kissing her hard, leaving his mark on her lips. "I hope you haven't unpacked. I'm taking you home."

"Why don't we go after some… er… time?" she asked, fluttering her eyelashes at him.

"Now I know the most fitting punishment for you, brat. NO! We are leaving right away."

"Are you sure you aren't punishing yourself as well?" she asked slyly, passing her overnight case to him.

"Don't know about myself. But I don't want your father to be punished any more than he has been. Let's go."

"Ouch!" Haasini turned sober on hearing his words. Shit! She had hurt her father all over again.

Vidyut went into Haasini's home along with her. Despite being way past midnight, most of the lights were on in her house.

"Dad! I'm sorry, Dad. Really, really, sorry. I don't have any excuse. Please forgive me." Haasini threw herself into her father's arms and begged him.

Phew!

Haresh met Vidyut's gaze above his daughter's head. "Rather you than me, my boy. Are you sure you still want to marry this troublesome young lady?" he asked.

Vidyut laughed, shrugging. "What to do, Uncle? I seem to have a penchant for only this brat."

"Hey, I'm right here. Why are you two talking over my head as if I don't exist?" Haasini scowled at them, or tried to.

"Why don't you get us all some coffee? I could definitely do with one," said Vidyut, arrogantly.

"With a shot of brandy, maybe?" asked Haresh, laughing.

The wonder was that Jyothi slept through all the adventure that night. The next morning, a much changed and humbled Janani faced her family. She felt truly ashamed of herself. To begin with, she berated herself: that she had behaved like the whore she had accused Haasini of being. She shuddered whenever she recalled the moment when she had jumped into Vidyut's lap. How horrible was that! It had taken the whole night, but she realised she had only herself to blame for everything and nobody else.

While it was true that Vidyut was handsome, Janani realised that he wasn't the man for her. And she had watched Vidyut and Haasini together. Without liking the fact, she accepted they were perfect for each other.

"I am sorry, Dad, Mom, Haasini. I have created a lot of trouble. Please forgive me."

Haresh turned to notice his elder child's embarrassed, red face. His heart melting, he pulled her into his arms and said, "Forget everything, Janani. Let us start afresh from today."

Haasini hugged her sister, her other arm around her mother, her eyes tearing up. After all, family was the foremost to the Cancer woman.

EPILOGUE

Haresh and Jyothi Rai conducted the weddings of both their daughters during the same *muhurta*. It was Vidyut who was more determined to find a suitable groom for Janani. He had found the perfect man in Nirmal's older brother, Rajesh Shetty, who had a senior job at an MNC, earning a potful of money month after month. It was a bonus that Rajesh was also good-looking and well-mannered. But then, Vidyut hadn't expected anything less from Nirmal's brother.

Jyothi shed joyous tears when she waved both her daughters goodbye; her hand on Haresh's arm. It was a major relief for the couple that the double-wedding had taken place without any untoward incident, considering their turbulent past.

Both Arun and Vandana were extremely happy to bring home Haasini as their daughter-in-law, adoring Vidyut's choice.

Avantika took one look at her brother's face and realised he was in love with the slender young woman he held at his side. "I'm so thrilled for you both, bro. Haasini is perfect for you. And I can see that you love her a lot."

"From the bottom of my heart," said Vidyut, grinning at his sister. "Though she leads me a fine dance," he continued in a loud whisper.

Avantika laughed when Haasini turned to grumble at her husband, "I heard that."

"I know you did, brat. Just as you were meant to," said a grinning Vidyut, kissing her on her nose.

Haasini blushed, catching not only her sister-in-law's eyes, but Avantika's husband, Shatrughan's, as well. "Stop it, Vidu. Everyone's watching," she grumbled some more, hiding her blushing face in his chest.

Shatrughan laughed, his arm around his wife's waist. "Don't mind us, peeps. We've been there, done that."

The two men bumped fists, laughing some more.

Vidyut and Haasini left for Singapore on a ten-day honeymoon the very next day, Arun and Nirmal promising to take care of the café during their absence. Haasini left her laptop at home as instructed by her husband; not keen to rile him. She realised she had tried the endurance of the ever-patient Taurus to the utmost limit.

But then, that's how crabs were. The Cancer needed re-assurance; wanting to be told she was loved, all the time, by all those around her.

"Love me?" she asked, opening her arms to him the morning after they reached their hotel.

"Hmm… let me see." Vidyut fell on the bed next to her, pretending to think hard, feeling her body vibrate in anger next to his own. Laughing, he turned to pull her into his arms, saying, "I love you totally, completely, absolutely, babe." He lowered his voice as he nuzzled her ear. "It's not that I cannot live without you. It's just that I *don't want to* live without you."

"Vidu!" Haasini choked on hearing his passionate words. "I love you too, sweetheart, with all my heart."

He pushed her on the bed to press his mouth to hers, drawing his tongue over the seam of her lips, smiling when he heard her sigh as she opened her mouth to draw his tongue within, sucking on it hungrily.

"Haasini…" He cupped her breasts in his hands, squeezing them, just the way she liked it. She wrapped her slender legs around his lean waist, guiding his manhood into her core.

She sighed some more when he pushed into her, filling her up before making love to her, thoroughly, until both were sated.

She hugged him close to her still thrumming body, burying her face into his neck; adoring her talking and walking Taurus Temptation.

THE END

References

1. https://www.docdroid.net
2. http://sunsignsbylindagoodman.blogspot.in
3. http://www.astro.com
4. https://www.self.com
5. http://horoscopes.lovetoknow.com

Bibliography

1. *Love Signs* by Linda Goodman

OTHER BOOKS
BY
SUNDARI
VENKATRAMAN

WRITTEN IN THE STARS
BOOK 1
SCORPIO
SUPERSTAR
SUNDARI
VENKATRAMAN
AMAZON BESTSELLING AUTHOR

SCORPIO SUPERSTAR
(Written in the Stars Book 1)

Kollywood superstar Chandrakanth, also known as CK, is a true-blue Scorpio, communicating with his eyes and believing in showing more than telling.

His website and social media consultant Ranjini is a Piscean through and through, fiercely independent.

It is love at first glance for Chandrakanth when he meets Ranjini; so strong are his feelings that he proposes marriage on their second meeting. Ranjini, fascinated by his starry persona, gets swept off her feet. The two get married without much of the world knowing—including CK's aunt and his ex.

The two women set out to settle their scores on Ranjini who suddenly begins to feel a strain in her fairy tale marriage.

While passion reigns on the one hand, there's trouble in paradise on the other. Although CK is by her side, the Scorpio in him expects her to trust him implicitly. But can the Pisces in Ranjini accept him at his word?

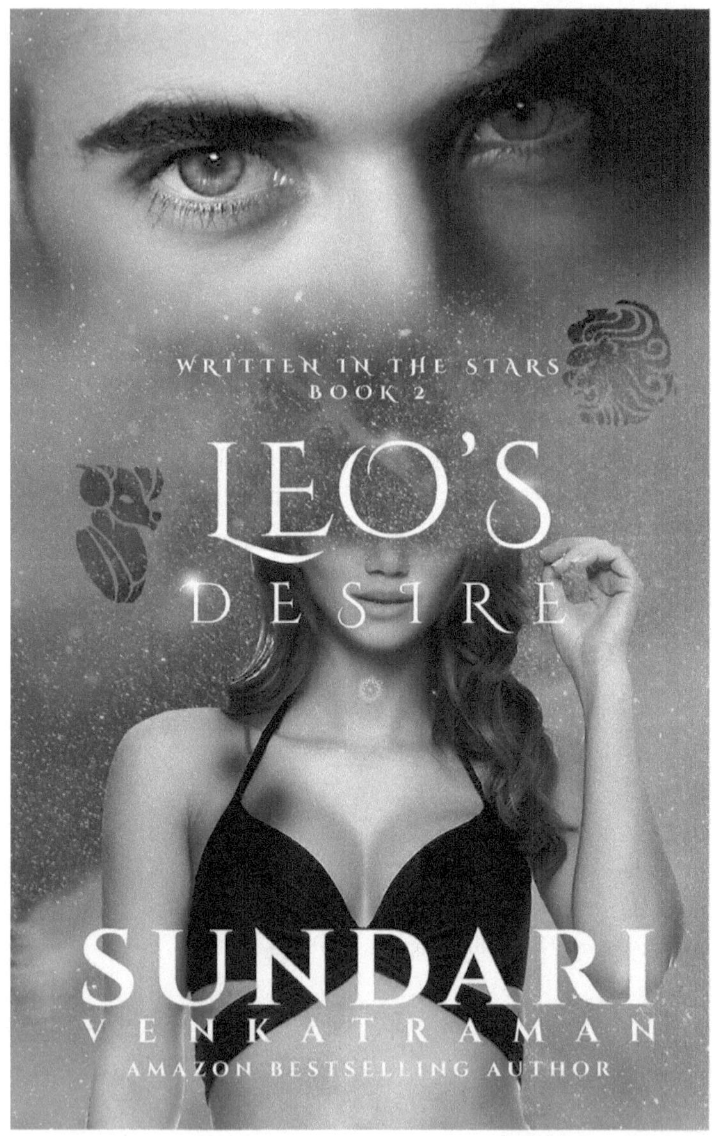

WRITTEN IN THE STARS
BOOK 2
LEO'S
DESIRE
SUNDARI
VENKATRAMAN
AMAZON BESTSELLING AUTHOR

LEO'S DESIRE
(Written in the Stars Book 2)

Twenty-four going on twenty-five, Nishaan Ahuja refuses to take life seriously. Intelligent and highly educated, he's slotted to become the Vice President of his father's multi-billion-rupee construction business. Only, the Leo man wants to live on his own terms. He takes the identity of Shaan and goes to work as a farm manager.

Chaahat finds a quick-fix cure to her plumpness as she's desperate to become a fashion model despite her parents' objections. The Aries woman is stubborn, determined and fiercely competitive. There's a hitch though. Her body refuses to cooperate as she continues to abuse it and she finds herself on the brink of a physical breakdown.

The Lion is a know-it-all and has to impart advice. Will the Lamb realise that it's all for her best?

Sparks fly in their love-hate relationship as Chaahat struggles to achieve her dreams with a lot of unsolicited help from Nishaan. Will the lovers be able to get together on their own terms, what with the distance which separates them; and their mammas doing their utmost to run interference?

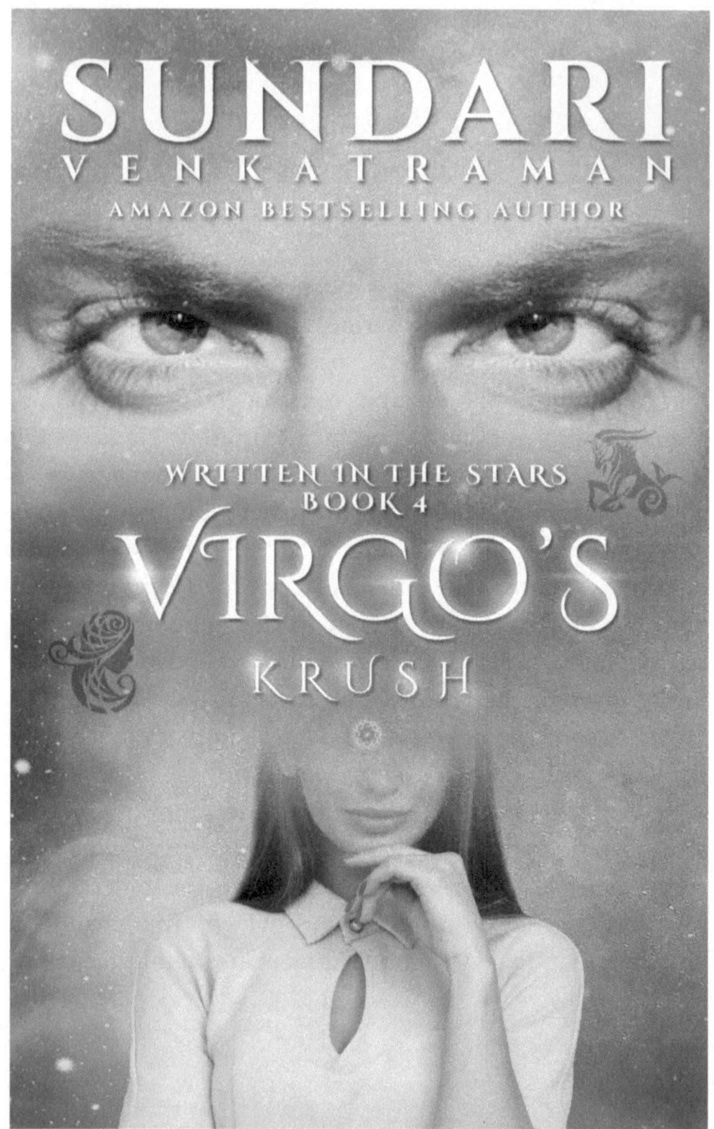

SUNDARI
VENKATRAMAN
AMAZON BESTSELLING AUTHOR
WRITTEN IN THE STARS
BOOK 4
VIRGO'S
KRUSH

VIRGO'S KRUSH
(Written in the Stars #4)

The gorgeous and intelligent Sanjana is a fiercely independent Virgo. Or is it only a front for the woman who wants to be loved?

As for Krish, the handsome and internationally famous photographer, is stunned to discover he is father to the two-month-old Kabir. Typically aware of his responsibilities, the Capricorn offers to marry the mother who he is deeply attracted to.

But the Virgo, already crushing on the Capricorn, wants all or nothing and refuses to settle for a loveless marriage.

He pushes, she resists...

It's like the proverbial Irresistible Force meeting the Immovable Object...

Shall the twain ever meet?

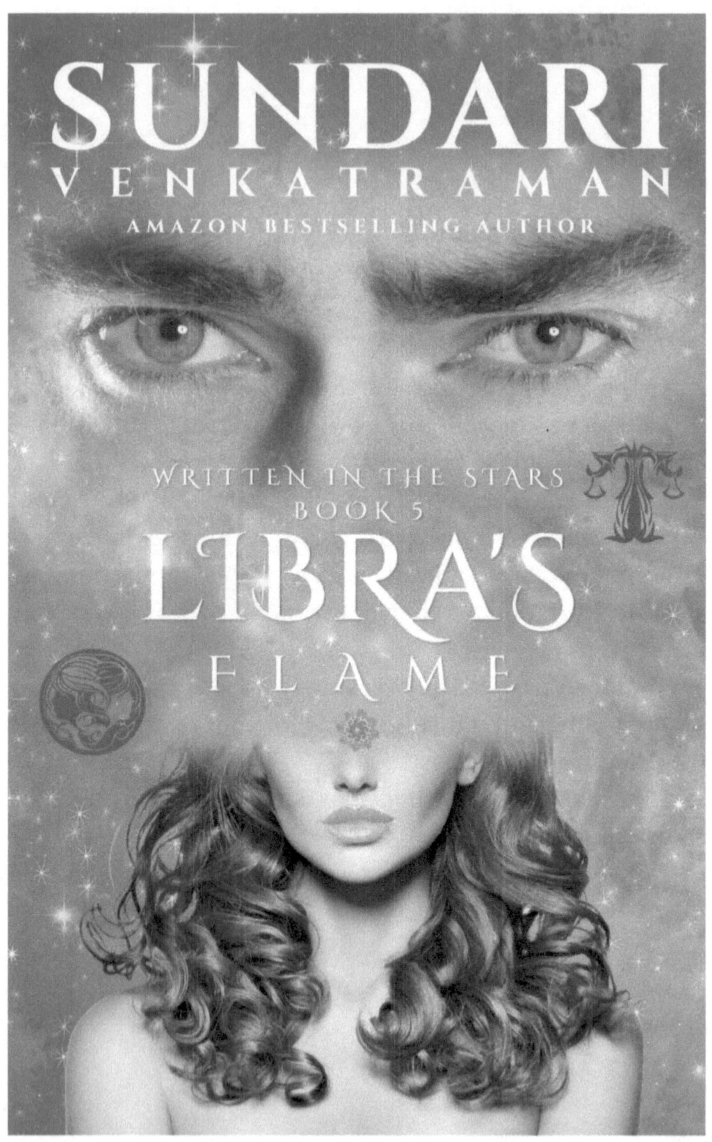

SUNDARI
VENKATRAMAN
AMAZON BESTSELLING AUTHOR
WRITTEN IN THE STARS
BOOK 5
LIBRA'S
FLAME

LIBRA'S FLAME
(Written in the Stars Book 5)

Dipika Sanyal is an established, internationally renowned business woman, running a modelling agency. She is swept off her feet by the handsome Mudit, who simply refuses to take 'no' for an answer. The Libra woman is completely floored from the word go.

Mudit Trivedi is the financial director of a multi-million crore business. He is deeply attracted to Dipika the moment he sets eyes on her. The Gemini does not want to wait for even a moment before getting to know her better.

Things go really well for the two in the beginning, until his estranged family enters the picture. Dipika has never met a ruder person than his father. Will their relationship survive the strain placed upon it?

Read the book to find out if this hot and sizzling pair of Libra and Gemini can have a life together.

SUNDARI
VENKATRAMAN
AMAZON BESTSELLING AUTHOR
WRITTEN IN THE STARS
BOOK 6
AQUARIUS
REBEL

AQUARIUS REBEL
(Written in the Stars #6)

*Y*oga instructor Shreya Udhas from Durban isn't at all interested in getting married, not when she's barely twenty-two. The Aquarius, who does not like conflict, is unable to stop her mother from going bridegroom hunting when they are holidaying in Delhi for a couple of months.

Chirag Bhatia runs an ad agency and is based in Delhi. The youngest of three siblings, the commitment-phobic Sagittarius is happy to let his older sisters provide the grandchildren for his parents to play with, while he himself prefers to lead the life of a fun-loving bachelor.

Sparks strike when they meet each other for the first time. And it isn't long before the Sagittarius guy and Aquarius gal enter a rocking affair. They don't even let the distance cramp their style over the next four years.

Until one day, Chirag receives Shreya's wedding invitation, to someone else. Shocked out of his wits, he's finally ready to admit to himself that he might be in love. But what if it is too late?

Connect with Sundari Venkatraman here:

Sundari Venkatraman Books

Sundari Venkatraman Books

https://www.sundarivenkatraman.in

Author Sundari Venkatraman

@sundarivenkat

@sundarivenkatraman

sundarivenkat@gmail.com